Lighthouse
on the
Lake

a birch harbor novel

ELIZABETH
BROMKE

LIGHTHOUSE ON THE LAKE

PUBLISHING IN THE PINES

White Mountains, Arizona

For Meagan.

Chapter 1—Amelia

One week.

That's how long it took to change her whole life.

One week.

Amelia had left Birch Harbor the previous Thursday. Now there she was, a whole seven days later, rolling back into town with her trusty sidekick, Dobi.

She patted the Dachshund's smooth potbelly as he panted on the musty upholstery beside her. Cigarette smoke clung to the interior of her loaner sedan, but the wind whipping through the cracked windows quelled the stench enough that she enjoyed the long drive. With the open road for a backdrop and daydreams for company, nothing stood between Amelia and her future.

Of course, the forty-something brunette had lots to do. Her first order of business, after Kate picked her up from the car rental agency that evening, was to get settled in her new room.

Or rather, her *old* room.

Amelia Hannigan was moving back into the house on the harbor. Although, it wasn't the house on the harbor anymore. The four sisters had settled on a new name for the future bed-and-breakfast, something befitting its emotional value and location on the quaint southern cove of the town in which they grew up.

They would call it *The Heirloom Inn*.

***

"Have you scheduled anything with Michael yet?" Kate asked once Amelia had finished returning her rental. The two women transferred the last of Amelia's boxes and garment bags to Kate's SUV.

Amelia had left New York with as little as she had arrived with. Spending the past decade or more traveling across America on her way to a starring role on Broadway had prevented her from accumulating much. Mostly just clothes and makeup, bedding and blankets (a Hannigan could never own too many throw blankets), and Dobi's various accessories.

As it turned out, Amelia was more vagabond than thespian, always searching for the next big role—or, as the case may have been—*any* role.

Still, despite all the rejection, she would never give up on her dream to be an entertainer.

It all started one summer in Arizona. The Hannigan girls spent a couple of months with an aunt who shuttled them around various desert tourist attractions. *Old Tucson Studios* proved to be the highlight for Amelia, who was at that time fourteen years old. There, they toured wild west movie sets and mined for fool's gold.

During a dusty gun show, the performers asked for a volunteer from the audience. Amelia's hand had shot up, and soon enough she slid from her hot bleacher seat and joined a Doc Holliday impersonator who instructed her to play along to a bank robbery. For the next fifteen minutes, Amelia darted in and out of wooden flats painted like Tombstone's infamous Allen Street. Her heart pounded in her chest; her face flushed.

After, she and her younger sister, Megan, sat and lapped up melting ice cream, giggling over the cute cowboy actors. Another visor-wearing tourist, her fanny pack slung low across high-waisted jean shorts, had stopped at the girls' table long enough to compliment Amelia's performance.

Since that day, the acting bug buzzed around inside of her like a fever.

But long years of traveling in pursuit of sporadic bit parts had steadily worn down her spirits. When she did get roles, nothing ever brought her to life quite like the historic reenactment.

When her mother, Nora, passed, Amelia realized how much she was looking forward to some stability. How much she was looking forward to being *home*.

Throwing her body against the back door of Kate's SUV, Amelia willed the uneven boxes to keep from spilling out long enough to make it just a few miles into town.

She let out a dramatic sigh at Kate's question about meeting Michael.

Michael Matuszewski was the Hannigan family lawyer, effectively. Amelia liked having a family lawyer. It felt prestigious. Aristocratic.

If only they *were* aristocratic, maybe then Amelia wouldn't even have to go on auditions. Maybe then she'd be offered leading parts merely because of her reputation as someone important. Connected.

In reality, Amelia had just received her most recent and crushing rejection: a coveted role as Lady Macbeth. And she'd ended things with her younger, more attractive boyfriend. And then her mom died.

Oh, yeah... *and* she'd sublet her New York studio in order to return home to Birch Harbor to help her older sister pull things together on the four—no, make that *five*—properties their mother's wobbly will had left in its wake.

Hers was not an aristocratic life, but that of a pauper. A commoner left to scrap together a living out of the shambles of a once hope-filled life.

Then again, perhaps having a claim to so many deeds did position the four Hannigan women in the upper echelon of small-town society, even if those properties were hodgepodge at best and ramshackle at worst. First, though, they'd need to shine the places up. It was one thing to own four places. It was another to own four *projects*. Oh, right. *Five*.

Amelia tucked Dobi onto her lap and stretched the seatbelt over her body. "Nothing formal, but Michael and I did text a little." She stared ahead but felt Kate's eyes on her. "*What?*" Amelia asked, flushing above her tunic before smiling at her older sister.

"Nothing. Nothing!" Kate replied and changed the subject. "So, Megan won't be in until this weekend at the *earliest*. Clara offered to come tomorrow after school. I have a couple ideas to get us started, but I didn't know whether we should meet with the lawyer first, or...?"

Kate was referring to the two big jobs that lay ahead of the Hannigan sisters. The renovation of the house on the harbor would first allow Kate and Amelia to take up residence there. Amelia suspected Kate intended on living in the oversized house for the long run, becoming a small-town innkeeper and hosting scores of tourists.

Amelia, however, saw a different future for herself. Though what, she didn't know.

Equally important to the reno project was to make sense of the recent revelation of the lighthouse.

In one of their mother's diary entries—the journal itself had yet to be unearthed—Nora Hannigan had vaguely referenced that the Birch Harbor Lighthouse would go to the girls, Amelia and her sisters.

As though the Hannigan estate wasn't complicated enough, the matter of the historic and abandoned property added a new layer of mystery.

The lighthouse had belonged to their father's parents, the Actons (yes—the Actons; Nora Hannigan never took her husband's name and instead forced a matrilineal tradition upon her daughters).

One would assume that upon the death of the Actons, ownership of the Birch Harbor monument would fall to their only son, Wendell Acton, the Hannigan girls' father.

But that was the problem. Wendell Acton had disappeared in 1992.

Chapter 2—Kate

Impatience thrummed beneath Kate's skin. She had grand plans for the Heirloom Inn, but this whole business regarding the lighthouse felt like a distraction.

Was it big news?

Yes.

Would they find answers about their father?

Maybe.

Was Kate interested in pursuing a man who'd left them high and dry over two decades earlier?

Not a chance.

They pulled up to 131 Harbor Avenue, the red house leaning into the sunset. Amelia had asked that they spend the evening getting settled first. Then, later, she would reach out to the lawyer and ask what needed to happen in order to open the conversation and proceedings regarding the Acton property.

"Here we are." Kate put the SUV into park and looked across to Amelia, who was studying the house through the windshield.

"Are you going to pull in?" Amelia gestured to the garage. The house had been built in the late 1800s and, originally, the secondary building functioned as a storage shed and boathouse. It may have even played barn to some animals, from Kate's understanding. Their mother converted it to a detached garage sometime in the nineties.

Kate answered, "No. It'll be too hard to unpack the SUV in that tight space." She glanced back at the sloppy piles of cardboard boxes towering at odd angles in the back seat and beyond. Amelia's life spread across the second row and filled the far back of the vehicle. A messy life—so very Amelia. Kate smiled. "Come on. Let's get something to eat. You must be starving."

Kate herself hadn't officially moved into the house on the harbor. She was still waiting to sell her home in the suburbs of Detroit. As a realtor, she intended to list it through the agency she worked for. Over the past week, Kate had taken four trips to and from Apple Tree Hill, the ample family home she'd shared with her late husband and their two sons who were currently away at college, shielded from their mother's big changes.

Slowly but merrily, Kate had begun bringing her personal effects to Birch Harbor. Furniture, appliances, and other big possessions would stay at Apple Tree Hill as staging for when the house hit the market.

But even without her furniture, Kate settled into her childhood room with surprising ease. Her old iron-frame bed still sat squarely beneath the window, thick lace curtains hanging heavily behind it. The lace managed to remain white thanks to a set of roman shades Nora had installed after Kate moved out for college.

Years earlier, Clara, the youngest of the Hannigan brood, had helped Nora drape *everything* in the house in dense white sheets. It was more a gesture of drama than one of practicality. Nora *should* have sold the furniture, maybe even the house.

Kate was glad she didn't.

On either side of the bed stood a wooden nightstand, though the left did not match the right. Kate had found them at the swap market in eighth grade and had scraped enough money together in order to negotiate with the seller. Later she asked her father to meet her at the corner of the entrance, where he kindly hefted them into the bed of his Toyota.

Once home, Nora had complimented Kate's choice. She liked that they didn't match. It would add character to her bedroom. But first, Nora admonished, she had to strip, sand, and stain the two pieces from tip to toe.

They'd sat in the barn, on the brink of rot, until Wendell Acton went in one day and handled the job, surprising Kate late that evening with the project. It had charmed Kate, and she remembered thinking her father was the type of man she would marry one day. She was certain of it.

But that was *before*.

***

"I've got a fruit platter and iced tea in the fridge and a frozen lasagna ready to pop in the oven. Are you still dieting, or can we throw some garlic bread in, too?" Kate cocked a suspicious eyebrow at Amelia, who threw up her hands.

"Bring on the carbs," Amelia declared, adding, "We can work it off later."

Kate grabbed the pitcher of tea from the fridge, and Amelia slid the fruit tray out behind her.

They situated the tray and the pitcher and two glasses on the table before lowering themselves onto the dated wooden chairs. Amelia reached for a round of kiwi, slipping it between her lips and puckering.

Grinning, Kate grabbed one for herself. It wasn't as sour as Amelia's face had suggested, but her mouth immediately watered around the sweet fruit. Her stare fixed on the wooden serving tray, a relic from their childhood.

"You know, Amelia, Mom left so much *stuff* here. And yet, the cottage is crowded with things, too."

Years earlier, when Nora decided the house on the harbor was too much work, or too full of memories, she left it to move inland, away from the water.

Before he'd left, Nora had asked their father to work on building a little cottage by Birch Harbor Creek. The Hannigan matriarch declared she wanted a second home where they could stow away after the birth of the youngest, Clara. At the time, Nora had felt it best to keep everything private, and the house on the harbor was decidedly a public venue, really. Wendell agreed easily and got to work right away, managing to make fast progress before he disappeared later in the summer.

When Nora and her daughters returned home from their extended vacation, not only was Wendell gone, but the house was incomplete.

It took some time until their mother found the help and the where-withal to get the project done. But she did, and the cottage would eventually become the home where she slipped from the earth into the ether, her soul finding its resting place in Heaven, Kate never doubted.

Despite the woman's hardness and searing work ethic, she loved her daughters. She loved her husband. Nora Hannigan had only ever done what she thought was best for them, even when the decision was wrought and twisted like a crooked iron gate. That's what Nora had done. She'd forged an impenetrable barrier between her family and the rest of the world. In her later years, once Clara had grown up, Nora began unlocking the gate, letting some people in and exploring the town for herself as a single woman. Single and heartsick. But no one in Birch Harbor knew how deep Wendell's absence had cut the steely-eyed Hannigan. As far as the town could see, Nora was a beautiful force who ran a severe household by day and joined in raucous Bunco games at the country club by night. An elegant and fun-loving divorcee, perhaps—though there had been no divorce between Nora and Wendell. At least, none that Kate was aware of.

"I think it's what happens," Amelia said.

"What do you mean?"

A sigh filled her younger sister's chest. Amelia took a sip of tea before replying. "When people age, they start clinging to the things that sort of... I don't know... tie them to Earth."

"They become collectors," Kate added thoughtfully.

Amelia nibbled on a sliced apple. "You know?" she asked between bites. "I suppose that was a good thing. I mean, sure, it's a lot of work. But look at this, Kate." She waved her arms around.

It was true. For all that Nora and Wendell lacked as parents—availability to help with homework, interest in volunteering at school or bringing sliced oranges to softball practice—they worked hard to leave their daughters a legacy.

Kate Hannigan intended to keep that legacy alive. She glanced around the kitchen, taking in a dated wooden spice cabinet, a butcher block for knives—each one rusty along where the blade disappeared into the handle, no doubt—and the hardy, rustic kitchen furniture and treatments.

The house on the harbor was going to be more than a little lakeside inn.

It was going to be a living history.

Grinning in agreement, Kate tugged a pad of paper and a pencil from the center of the table to the space in front of her. "You're right. Now let's talk inn-keeping."

Chapter 3—Clara

The final bell rang, and Clara Hannigan fell into her desk chair, momentum rolling her back into the window.

Teaching was draining. Emotionally, physically, and mentally draining. But she loved it. It would be good if she strode out with the kids, keeping an eye over them as they rushed down the hall and out toward the busses and their waiting parents. Teachers were supposed to reign over teenage hormones at every moment, but Clara needed to be in her classroom just then, away from the chaos. It was a mental health choice.

She stared out the window which featured a view to the back of the school. Few students left that way—only those with parents who worked in one of the school buildings, since it was the faculty and staff parking lot. Most spilled out the front doors, automatically veering to one of the two busses that sat waiting or beyond to the parent pickup line. Anyone who lived within a mile or had plans to be at a friend's house within a mile or so, simply left on foot, braving the onslaught of summer tourists in order to make it home.

Of the high schoolers from the secondary building, the ratio was sharper, with many walking or driving themselves away from campus.

In Birch Harbor, fewer students rode busses, with only a fraction packing themselves onto the hot plastic seats, terrorizing each other and the bus driver for up to sixty minutes of a jagged route that heaved and hoed around town.

The rest tucked themselves into SUVs and minivans, walked, or drove themselves away from the ancient brick building that sat just inland from Harbor Avenue, off a small side street called Lowell. On the other side of Lowell sprawled the Birch Harbor Cemetery. No one seemed to mind that you could learn the Pythagorean Theorem, then go visit Granny in one fell swoop. It was one of those quirks of a small town, charming and bizarre to outsiders, normal and mundane to insiders.

The image of an errant student caught Clara's eyes. A girl from one of her classes—Mercy Hennings—with her head down, hands gripping the polyester straps of her backpack as she strode languidly toward a waiting truck.

Clara looked more closely at the man standing outside of the truck, his hands shoved into jean pockets.

She'd met Mercy's father just once, the week before, in fact. He was kind and grateful, the ideal parent. Easygoing and casual, Mr. Hennings was the polar opposite of his daughter, whose anxiety and seriousness aligned more closely with Clara's own personality.

She felt like a voyeur, watching them hug in the parking lot. The father kissed Mercy's head. She passed him her backpack, then they lifted themselves into either side of the truck. A happy duo.

Clara felt a pang in her heart.

She'd never been kissed by her father. Not once in her life.

***

Half an hour later, Clara called her oldest sister.

Kate answered her phone breathlessly. "Hey."

"How's it going?" Clara asked, munching on a baggie of baby carrots as she slid into the front seat of her car.

"Good, good. We decided to get Amelia's room cleaned out and set up. Then we'll meet with Michael. I think Amelia is waiting on him to call her back."

A second voice floated past in the distance of the phone call. Clara knew it was Amelia's. She and Kate exchanged muffled words, then Kate came back on the line. "Sorry, I mean Amelia is definitely *not* waiting on him to call her back. They are texting, I guess. I don't know why, but it's all very hush-hush." Kate laughed lightly, but Clara frowned. She was sick of things being hush-hush, even if it was a jokey hush-hush.

Clara stalled at the mouth of the parking lot. "Should I come over now or... I mean what's the plan for tonight?"

"Come over as soon as you're ready. Our goal is to finish Amelia's room and the bigger bathroom on the second floor. Then, we're laying out a game plan."

Dedicated to being part of the team, Clara replied that she was on her way. After all, there was something she'd like to add to the supposed *game plan*.

***

When she arrived at the house on the harbor, a sense of doom settled over her. In the years that her three older sisters had lived away, Clara had been the lone Hannigan responsible for keeping the house on the harbor in acceptable shape.

It was a job she was not made for. Clara was not a fix-it-upper type. She was a grade-papers type or a jigsaw-puzzle-doer type. Still, for as long as she and her mother had lived away from the big house on Heirloom Cove, Clara watered the plants and even sometimes did a little yard work. She conducted walk-throughs of the property from time to time, ensuring no one had broken in and vandalized. But that was it. Clara did not live her life in the shadow of the family's past. At least, insomuch as was possible.

Now, she wondered what it might be like to return to the fold. Would she find a new joy in scrubbing dated toilets and changing old bed sheets?

Probably not.

But she *would* find joy in bonding with her sisters. After all, being over ten years younger, Clara had never really gotten that chance.

Chapter 4—Megan

"I won't leave for Birch Harbor until Saturday, Brian. We still have tomorrow to file. I'm not running away from the *divorce*." The word stuck in her throat like gum. Megan swallowed. "I can promise you that." Exasperated and tired, she rubbed the back of her neck with her hand.

Megan Stevenson stood at her kitchen island facing her soon-to-be-ex-husband, who compulsively tapped his thumb on the granite.

"The attorney's office is *closed* on Fridays, Megan," he shot back, his Adam's apple bobbing below a five o'clock shadow. "I mean it's fine by me if we push it out, but you're the one who was anxious to get the ball rolling."

Before, Megan had always loved it when Brian skipped a few days of shaving. He looked good with a dark shadow across his lower face. It added a rugged edge to his otherwise intellectual affect. He adjusted the glasses on his nose and blinked.

She looked away. "It doesn't matter. We don't need the lawyer to file, Brian. We have the paperwork, and we agreed to list the house. All we have to do is turn everything in. And—" Megan licked her lips. Her neck flushed, and her chest tightened.

"And you're done." Their teenage daughter, Sarah, had entered the room, her phone dangling in her hand by her side. Her eyes watered, and her voice trembled. "So, you're really going through with it?" the girl asked, though it came out more like a plea.

Megan and Brian exchanged a look. He held her gaze, his eyebrows lifted above the rims of his glasses, his lips parted. It was the same look he would give her when they were in the middle of a heated argument, like he was waiting for the moment that everything would go back to normal and they could hug and make up.

She squeezed her eyes shut. "Can we just... can we just revisit this next week?"

It was a bold suggestion. The matter was drawing out week after week. First, with Brian's stalling on whether he wanted to accept her offer of the house in exchange for alimony. Then he waffled on even that. Now it was her turn to find a reason for delaying proceedings.

Brian nodded, and if Megan didn't know any better, she thought a smile flickered on his lips. "Yes, please. That's better. I would hate to... rush things."

Her breath caught in her throat, but she pushed it out. "Right. Well, I have to go to the lake this weekend. I'll be back Monday. Do you want to go?" The question was for Sarah, but for some reason, Megan's eyes lingered on Brian as she said it.

He waited a beat, then turned on his heel and left the room, his eyes glued to his phone. Megan simply shook her head and pinned Sarah with a stare. "Do you?" she pressed.

"Um, actually I had a party to go to this weekend."

Megan's shoulder fell in. "No. No parties. Especially while I'm gone."

"Mom," Sarah protested, pouting.

An idea materialized in Megan's mind. "No. Actually, I think you *will* come with me. It'll be fun. I promise." With a wry grin, she folded her arms over her chest and nodded at her daughter.

"Come on," the teenager huffed, spinning on her heel and stomping away and up the stairs.

But Megan didn't care. Summer was beginning, and she figured there was no better way to start than with a girls' weekend. Besides, maybe Clara would be willing to share her big news with her "niece."

***

"We're on our way," Megan chirped through the Bluetooth to Kate.

She could hear Kate's smile through the car speaker. "Is Sarah with you?"

"Yep." Megan flashed a knowing look to her daughter, who was too busy shuffling through her social media apps to notice. It was just as well. Megan wasn't sure she could handle any more attitude from the high school junior. Or rather, almost-senior.

"Kate," Megan went on, adjusting her grip on the steering wheel. "What's the latest with the lighthouse? Has Amelia met with Michael Matuszewski yet?"

"No. They've been in touch, but nothing firm is set. I'm really hoping we can just focus on the *Inn first*."

Megan frowned. "What do you mean 'focus on the *Inn*' first?"

"The house on the harbor. You know... The Heirloom Inn?"

"Yeah, I know. I mean, is there some sort of rush, or—"

"Well," Kate answered, her voice growing quieter. "It's just... Let's talk about everything when you get here. Okay?"

Megan ended the call and focused on the drive. Knowing her family, there was also something else looming on the horizon. A secret. A scandal. Gossip.

Maybe it wasn't such a great idea to bring Sarah along after all.

Chapter 5—Amelia

Heavy clouds converged overhead as Amelia and Kate helped Megan and Sarah with bringing their bags into the house—or, as Kate continued to insist on calling it, the *Inn*.

The air was thick with the threat of rain, and Amelia hoped Clara showed up soon, too. It was time to get the party started. Literally. Amelia had spent the previous evening stocking up on snacks and goodies. She fully intended to pull together a pseudo housewarming party for herself and Kate, who was none the wiser so far.

Once everyone was inside, Kate immediately took to the windows, cranking them open and inhaling with great drama while Amelia conducted Megan and her daughter upstairs to Megan's old room.

As soon as they were up and unpacking, Amelia shooed Kate to the front to wait for Clara. "I have a little surprise," Amelia whispered conspiratorially.

Kate threw her a skeptic glance but followed directions, tapping at her phone as she sashayed to the parlor windows, which she dutifully stretched open.

It was too warm out to have the windows open, but the air conditioner was broken anyway, and they meant to air the place out the night before but had grown too tired to remember to open the downstairs windows. Thankfully, the storm would cool the place off, no doubt.

Amelia unpacked her hitherto hidden grocery sacks, arranging the goodies in charming baskets she'd discovered in the pantry.

Then, she lined the treats artfully along the center of the island and pulled a bottle of champagne and a jug of orange juice she'd managed to stash in the far back of the fridge. After rinsing and drying five delicate glass flutes, she angled them in little rows and fanned out a pack of green paper napkins beside the white plates she'd stacked at the far end of the island.

Glancing suspiciously into the foyer, she saw that Kate had left through the front door and was thoroughly distracted by the arrival of Clara. Amelia tugged her phone loose from her back pocket and scrolled to her music app, finding a station and hitting play before setting the device in a ceramic mixing bowl. The trick worked, and a bright ballad carried nicely from the makeshift acoustic station, echoing around the kitchen in pretty reverberation.

As one final touch, Amelia dug beneath the countertop into a narrow cabinet, finally withdrawing a vase of buttery yellow daffodils. She'd have chosen dahlias, but they weren't nearly as bright, and that weekend demanded positive spirits. After all, the Hannigan women were embarking on a new beginning.

Amelia caught a glimpse of the door opening and closing, and so she dashed out, wiping her hands along the front of her jeans. "Clara!" she beamed, holding her hands out and wiggling her fingers until she'd lured the petite blonde into her arms.

Clara hugged Amelia back, and then they pulled apart. Amelia felt that she was seeing her youngest sister in a new light. Clara seemed refreshed. Her face was flushed, and a smattering of light freckles spread from her nose to her cheeks. Amelia didn't remember Clara having freckles. While Kate, Amelia, and Megan were aging, their baby sister was glowing.

"You look great," Amelia gushed, then added suspiciously, "Why?"

Kate and Clara laughed together, but Clara came up with an answer, much to Amelia's surprise. "I feel like I can breathe for the first time in a long time."

Amelia crooked her head. "What do you mean?"

"Taking care of Mom was exhausting, you know? And I miss her. I miss her so much. But, well—" she looked at Kate with affection, and Amelia knew exactly what she meant.

"We've talked a lot," Kate interjected, squeezing Clara's shoulder. "All good things. Now that I'm going to live here full time, I think

Clara and I—*and you*," she stabbed a finger at Amelia, "can finally catch up."

Kate was right. Fourteen years Clara's senior meant that Amelia was out of the house before Clara even knew how to read. The age gap felt insurmountable when they were younger. But it was closing. Especially now that the three of them were back in Birch Harbor. Together.

"Okay, you two go upstairs and get Megan and Sarah. I'll wait in the kitchen for you," Amelia said, propping her hands on her waist. Though she was anxious to get into Michael's office and discuss the lighthouse, it felt good to save the weekend for her sisters—and niece.

After all, the Hannigans hadn't enjoyed much girl time in recent years.

She strode to the kitchen, taking in the sweet and simple scene: baskets of chocolate and a little plate of meats and cheeses, the mimosa fixings, and the fresh flowers converged into something picturesque. For a brief moment, Amelia saw exactly what Kate was envisioning for the place.

A quaint bed-and-breakfast, complete with midmorning snacks and afternoon tea, maybe. Sherry in thick crystal goblets in the parlor before dinner. Tourists from all over the country—*no*, the *world*. There, in their family home, enjoying Lake Huron and Birch Harbor as tourists do—with admiration and delight.

Amelia wondered if she ought not just pretend the lighthouse didn't exist. Maybe her place was there, in the Heirloom Inn, among her family and whatever visitors arrived for a cozy weekend getaway.

Then again, no. That wasn't Amelia. She wasn't a hostess ushering people into a dinner theatre show.

Amelia-Ann Hannigan was the main act.

And she needed a real venue.

Chapter 6—Kate

"Welcome home!"

Kate opened her eyes and unhooked her arm from Clara's. She smiled and clasped her hands together. "Oh, Amelia," Kate squealed. Kate Hannigan *never* squealed. Here she was, though. In her childhood home with her sisters and her niece, and she was *squealing*. "How precious is this?" she cried, striding to the kitchen island. "Are we... celebrating?" Kate asked Amelia.

"Yes, we're celebrating. We're home. We're moving in. We're opening a business. It's a housewarming party and a business meeting and whatever we want it to be. I figured I'd pull out all the stops." Amelia wriggled her eyebrows at Kate, who laughed at her younger sister's typical exorbitance.

"Mimosas and chocolate and daffodils? You've spoiled us." Kate rounded the island and slipped an arm around Amelia's waist, tugging her into a hug.

Megan and Sarah stepped into the kitchen after Kate. Sarah raised an eyebrow pointedly at the champagne. "Can I—?"

"No," Megan answered as quickly as Sarah formed the question and then pretended to pinch her daughter's cheek as she grabbed the bottle and started to work on removing the foil. "Amelia, I'm impressed, and I'm grateful. I think this is just what we needed."

Kate looked at Amelia, who beamed in reply and rocked onto her heels as she tucked her hands into her jeans pockets. Kate felt a sisterly pride creep in. She sneaked a look at Clara, who was lifting a bloom to her nose. "These are so fresh, Amelia. Did you get them at the Lakeside Market?"

Amelia wagged a finger. "Nope. I mean, I went there for the grub and drinks, but I made a special trip to White Birch Floral for these babies." Amelia ran a hand gently up the full bouquet, bouncing the blooms along her fingers. Kate winced a little.

"Sparing no expense, I see," Megan murmured just before a loud *pop* scared them all half to death.

Kate caught Sarah roll her eyes (in true teenage fashion) before the girl plucked a slice of watermelon and perched on a stool. Kate pressed a hand to her chest. "I hate loud corks," she declared and then selected a flute and tipped it toward Megan who wasted no time in filling four of the five glasses. The fifth glass she filled with pure orange juice and passed to her daughter.

"I'd like to make a toast," Kate announced, raising her pale-yellow drink. A breeze curled in from the kitchen window behind them, sending a chill up Kate's spine. She smiled.

The others followed Kate's gesture, even Sarah with her chaste glass of OJ.

Kate cleared her voice, preparing for the cascade of tinkling. Pressing her champagne flute above the center of the island, she announced, "To the Heirloom Inn."

***

An hour later, after listening with rapt horror as Sarah recounted various tales of high school terror (with Clara nodding along in somber confirmation), the women had polished off the last of the cheese and watermelon. A few rounds of limp deli meat clung to the sides of their plastic tray. Every last glass was empty, but the champagne bottle still held a dignified amount of liquid.

Kate's stomach lurched from overindulging. She let out a long sigh. "All right. I suppose it's time to get down to business." Kate clapped her hands on her thighs and rose, reaching for plates and carrying them dutifully toward the white porcelain sink. Its apron splayed over the front like a modern farmhouse, although that was never Nora's intent. She'd hoped to one day upgrade to stainless steel everywhere in the kitchen. But other things came first. Bigger projects. All this meant that the poor woman died happy. Happy or smug. That's how Kate felt when fashion or decor rounded the eras, plopping back in style decades later. Smug. *Acid wash jeans were in style when I was younger than you*, she'd told one of her sons' girlfriends when she spied a high-rise pair the prior summer. She thought it might mark her as some surprising combination of wise and hip. Instead, she sounded like an old fart.

Oh well.

Kate wasn't concerned about appearing trendy. She was not a trendy sort of person. But she did consider herself stylish. Even acquaintances and strangers had sometimes remarked on Kate's ability to pull off simple, chic "looks." This always made her smile. Kate had never been as classically beautiful as Amelia or Megan. And surely she wasn't cute like Clara.

With a stout build and a long Roman nose, Kate was more tomboy than fashion model. But even so, she was selective with accessorizing. Unlike her mother, whose knuckles clacked with gaudy jewels and whose chest shone with oversized gems, Kate preferred the less-is-more theory. A few clever basics were enough to transform her from a homely, broad-shouldered empty-nester into a respectable modern woman. With a sleek blonde A-line bob cutting crisply across the very tips of her shoulders and smart-looking tortoise-shell glasses, all it took was a swipe of red lipstick and a starched white button-down to turn her into something more than a widowed mother and a part-time realtor. And, with her latest project underway, Kate felt that she was emerging into a new, grand phase. The one that came after raising children and playing subordinate to her husband and the few bosses she'd known. Now, Kate Hannigan was a small-town business owner. An *innkeeper*.

Chapter 7 — Clara

Kate had given them each a neatly printed list of to-dos. Everything from a rotation of linen-laundering to toilet-scrubbing to baseboard-wiping was accounted for and assigned. Even poor little Sarah earned a position as window-washer.

Clara was excited to spend time with her niece. Maybe she'd even work up the courage to open the conversation she hadn't yet had with her extended family members, not even Megan's daughter.

But first, before anyone began on her assignment, Kate asked for help in making some "big-picture decisions," as she called them.

Clara smiled at her, admiring the woman's togetherness and dedication. Rehabbing and opening the house as a bed-and-breakfast was the perfect opportunity for Kate, Clara knew.

A dry erase board appeared out of nowhere, and Kate lifted a chubby Expo marker and added the words *The Heirloom Inn* to the top then drew a perfectly straight line beneath.

"All right," she began, her hands steepled like she was running a business meeting. Clara supposed she was. "Upstairs, there are six rooms. Three of those rooms have closets. Three do not."

They all knew as much; the older three had fought to the death over who would get the closet spaces. In the end, Nora had decided that Kate, Amelia, and Megan would each get a room *without* a closet. It was the fairest approach. This meant that when Clara was born and a room was dedicated to her, it was a closet room. She secretly suspected her older sisters had long begrudged her that. Now, it was a silly thing. Then again, regarding the whole establishment of a bed-and-breakfast, a closet might be more significant after all: it could mean the difference in price points for guest rooms. Clara frowned and leaned in.

As if reading her mind, Megan interjected. "Charge more for bedrooms with closets."

"What about Mom and Dad's old room?" Amelia asked, glancing around. "It's the biggest. Will one of us get it, or...?"

Kate pinned Amelia with a look. "Good question. I suppose that depends on *your* long-term plans *and mine*," she replied.

Clara felt her stomach clench in anxiety. This was the conversation they'd been having since Nora passed. Who would get what? Who was getting too much? Too little? It was the precise reason Clara was happy to begin moving into the cottage. A small, separate space, private and all her own. And, detached from the house or the rental units. Clara felt lucky to get the cottage, and that was exactly why she was waiting for the other shoe to drop and one of her sisters to protest about fairness.

Amelia cleared her throat. "Listen, Kate," she began, looking around at the others guiltily. "I love being here. And I'll stay for a while. But sharing this place with tourists? Not my bag. I'm not in it for the long run. I may not even stay in Birch Harbor past the summer, honestly." She shrugged.

Kate lowered her gaze to Amelia. "I understand. And I *will* be here for the long run." She shot Clara a small smile.

Curious, Clara pressed her on it. "You're going to stay *here* long term?" She indicated the house by twirling her index finger in a little circle.

A broad grin took over the woman's face. "I know that we have to keep this place going. And I'm the oldest. I'm the one who's most interested. So yes, I plan to stay for a while."

With that settled, they quickly began assigning placements and establishing parameters.

"I'll move into Mom and Dad's room. It has the en suite bath and sits at the far side of the hall. The other five rooms will be guest rooms. But, what about all of you?" Kate paused, looking at her sisters.

"You mean where will we stay when we come to town?" Megan asked.

Kate nodded.

Clara felt her cheeks flush. She didn't want to share the cottage. But if it were just for Megan and Sarah, she could do it. "You'll stay with me," she answered for Kate. "Whenever you want, you can stay in the cottage with me, once I move in. Until then, we will bunk together in my unit at The Bungalows."

Sarah spoke up, excitement in her voice. "Yes! That's perfect," she cheered, grinning at Clara affectionately. It felt good to have the girl's admiration. Really good.

"Wonderful. That's wonderful!" Kate pushed ahead. "And in the long run, we can have the attic converted. Or even the basement! If we work hard, we could have beds in both before autumn." She added notes to the white board—*second-floor guest rooms: five.*

Clara chimed in. "What about bathrooms? There are just two others than the en suite upstairs. Can five guest rooms work with just two bathrooms?"

"We have one down here, too," Amelia added helpfully.

Kate frowned deeply.

Clara licked her lips. "Maybe that's okay, you know? Not all bed-and-breakfasts have individual bathrooms. Sometimes you have to share with your floor or whatever. Like a college dorm."

"You don't have much competition in town," Megan said. "But eventually you want to offer the best experience, right? You want to beat out Birch Harbor Motel, right?"

"Right," Kate answered.

Clara studied Megan, her features bare of makeup, her hair tossed up in a messy bun. For over-forty, she looked good for her age. It was no wonder Sarah was so beautiful. She closely resembled her mom. Dark hair and bright green eyes against olive skin. Clara knew they looked nothing like Nora. Did they look like Nora's husband? Wendell Acton? She frowned for a moment, then a thought occurred to her.

"I've got it." Clara's eyes lit up, and she snapped her fingers. "For now, just rent out two bedrooms upstairs. The ones by each hall bath. Build up some savings, then we can convert the basement and add two rooms down there with two new baths. That saves the first-floor bath as a main level powder room, and it gives you time to work your way up to a full-service bed-and-breakfast."

Kate nodded excitedly.

"Full-service? You make it sound like a brothel," Amelia joked. Clara didn't laugh. Amelia did, though. Sarah rolled her eyes.

"Anyway," Kate cut through Amelia's laughter. "I love that idea, Clara. We can ease in. It's perfect."

The window behind them illuminated in a bright boom of lightning. A crack of thunder erupted through their conversation. Then, like a scene from a movie, rain spilled from the sky, pattering on the back porch loudly as the sky lit up in a fresh flash of lightning. A Saturday morning storm in late May. Clara's favorite weather, even if it mismatched the tone of their little party. A cool breeze splashed through the screen door behind the kitchen island, tickling Clara's neck and reminding her how warm the house was.

"First," Clara remarked. "You'd better look into having the air conditioning unit serviced." She gave Kate a helpless look, but Kate already knew this and nodded back, twisting her mouth into a thoughtful pout.

"And paint," Megan added. "The exterior is peeling off in swaths," she said.

Again, Kate nodded and then narrowed her eyes on an absent focal point in the distance. "We need to hire someone," she said, sighing deeply. "Someone who can help with *all* of this. Or maybe several *someones*. I'm not sure we can manage alone."

"I know someone," Clara answered, a timid smile dancing on her lips.

Kate frowned and stared at her. "Okay. Well, who?"

Clara's smile turned to a grimace as she answered. "Your ex-boyfriend."

Chapter 8—Megan

Now organized into pairs, Megan and Kate got to work. Since Kate had already vacuumed and mopped the common area floors and oiled the banisters and furniture, they could turn their attention to the two guest rooms upstairs, focusing on cleaning and making notes for decor.

Clara and Sarah set about the windows with a secondary task to head up the laundry cycles.

Amelia worked independently on the upstairs bathrooms, blasting music out of her phone like an obstinate teenager. Typical Amelia.

Kate told Megan she also wanted help with establishing a check-in desk of some sort. Last on her list was to tackle the kitchen, but Megan convinced her that she was biting off more than she—or any of them—could chew in one weekend.

As they set about stripping the bed and collecting old trinkets from around the room and boxing them up, Megan asked Kate what her timeline was.

"What do you mean?" Kate replied.

Megan tugged the bed skirt loose from its wedge between the box spring and mattress. "When are you going to start advertising? When are you going to open for business?"

Kate sighed. "Well, I'm listing my Apple Tree Hill house in a week or two. Once that's on the market, I'd like to get everything moved here, to the basement or attic for now, I suppose. Then, I'll be able to focus *all* of my energy on the Inn."

"Plus, you need to call Matt, right?" Megan pointed out, tossing the wadded white lace-trimmed bedding into the hallway.

Blinking, Kate's face flushed. "Or whoever can help, yes."

"Why not Matt?" Megan pushed. Matt Fiorillo was Kate's high school boyfriend. They'd reconnected in the wake of the funeral and over the drama with Clara from a week ago, but Megan could tell things were still tepid, at best. She wondered why. If Megan was skillful at one thing in life, it was identifying a good match. Her sister and the Birch Harbor house-flipper were a good match. They had that origin story that so few couples have. High school sweethearts. Grave drama. Dire straits. Distance. And then, a second-chance meeting, years later.

"I mean I'll call him, but he might not want to help. Maybe he's too busy." Kate left the room with the banker's box tucked under her arm. Megan followed her.

"You're afraid," Megan trilled as they strode down the hall, Megan with a pile of musty-smelling bedding resting in her arms.

They passed Amelia and her loud music and descended the stairs, veering through to the lower staircase that would take them into the basement.

Once they were down there and Megan was stuffing her wad of whites into the empty washing machine, Kate shelved the box of doo-dads and faced Megan, crossing her arms severely over her chest.

Megan poured detergent and fabric softener into the little drawers, punched them closed, and set the machine. Ignoring Kate's pout, she commented, "I thought Clara and Sarah were running laundry."

"They are," Kate replied, her eyes narrowing on Megan.

"Then let's get back upstairs and vacuum the mattress or whatever neurotic thing you do when you clean." There it was. Megan crossed a line.

Kate audibly sucked in a breath then unleashed on Megan. "You think I'm afraid to call Matt. I've been talking to Matt all week! I'm not *afraid* to talk to him. If anyone in this house is afraid of something, it's *you*." She jabbed a finger at Megan. A distinct shift in tone unmoored Megan from her stance on the cold concrete floor.

"Whoa, whoa, whoa," Megan held up her hands in an innocent plea. "I didn't mean to set you off. What are you *talking* about?" she shot back.

"Megan, look at you. You have a good husband, and you're pulling the plug. And why? Because he never pushed you to get a career? Because he was focused on his own? News flash, sis, we are all focused on ourselves." She shook her head and uncrossed her arms, raising them helplessly. "I don't understand you. None of us do. Brian is a good guy. Why end it?"

Megan's throat closed up immediately. Her heart started to burn in her chest. She felt the instant urge to chew up half a bottle of Tums. Megan was *not* about to open this conversation. Not in the middle of a girls' weekend with her sisters during what ought to be a fun project. A healing project. "Are you serious?" she asked, searching for a way to end the line of questioning.

"Yes, I'm serious. You're here pointing a finger at me, suggesting I am afraid of initiating... *something* with Matt Fiorillo. Meanwhile, you're leaving your own marriage. So, what is it with you, Megan? Do you believe in love or not?"

Blinking back the threat of tears, Megan was desperate to push past Kate and storm upstairs and out through the front doors. Never to look back.

But she was better than that.

"Of course I believe in love," she admitted at last, her face crumbling and her body slumping into relief and defeat. Then, as she felt Kate's arms wrap around her, Megan added, breathlessly, "I still love Brian."

"Then why are you leaving him?" Kate whispered back.

Megan swallowed the lump in her throat and quelled her crying long enough to find an answer. "I don't know anymore."

Chapter 9—Amelia

The rest of the weekend went well. Better than well, even. They'd managed to handle a significant portion of the cleaning. Amelia was pleased to go to bed the night before knowing they'd cleared out and set up one guest room, one hall bath, and even tackled the kitchen, not to mention some other wide-scale jobs like the interior windows and rounds and rounds of laundry.

Sometime around four in the morning, Kate crept into Amelia's room, who sensed her sister before she saw or heard her. Neither of them could sleep. The buzz of excitement and new beginnings grew palpable, and once Kate's face appeared in the milky twilight at Amelia's bedside, they shared a grin like a pair of schoolgirls at a slumber party.

So, instead of sleeping, Amelia untucked herself from the narrow bed and followed Kate to the kitchen where they brewed a pot of coffee and sat by the window. The tug of exhaustion pulled hard beneath Amelia's eyes, and she knew that come afternoon, she'd be dragging, but it was interesting to rise before the sun for once.

For so many years Amelia had lived her life in the night, rather than the morning, waking well past noon to tend to Dobi's needs, shower, get dressed and ready for her evening waitress shift. After, she would lamely follow her younger friends on their playful journey to the cheapest show of the night. Then, even later, Amelia would tag along for some party where she was out of place and generally miserable. She'd last until two or three until she begged off and trudged home on foot or by subway, reeking of body odor and cigarettes by the time she plopped onto her creaky bed with eager Dobi, too tired and depressed to bother with a bath. Too tired and depressed to mind that Dobi had filled his little potty pad to the brim.

Typically, the next morning, the raunchy cycle would replicate itself, and Amelia would begin her day with high hopes for something new to come her way—starting with a fresh potty pad and a shower hot enough to sear away the bad decisions. Some days she'd take Dobi on long, inspiring walks and talk herself into a new plan. But it failed each time, and each day she slipped back into a New York rut.

Then, her mom died.

And once one's mom dies, everything changes.

So it was with Amelia and little Dobi.

As the second-oldest Hannigan sat in silence with a tuckered-out Dobi snuggled on her lap watching the sun rise, she wondered if it was only possible to start over if you were pushed to it.

She asked Kate as much.

"What do you mean?" her sister replied, tearing her eyes away from the window.

Amelia let out a deep sigh. "If Mom hadn't died, would I wait tables for the rest of my life? Would I have held out for a good role for another twenty or thirty years, pretending I wasn't the oldest one at the restaurant all the while?"

Kate chuckled and drew a sip of her coffee. "It's been one weekend since you moved. Who knows if you aren't still destined for that?"

Bristling, Amelia replied, "You think it's my *destiny* to be miserable?"

"No. Of course not. And anyway, Mom would have died one day. If she were immortal, we'd have other issues."

Amelia allowed herself a laugh despite feeling a little hurt. "Really, Kate. Do you think I am destined to be miserable and wait tables all my life?"

Kate set her mug down with purpose and shifted in her seat, looking directly into Amelia's eyes. "I think you're in charge of your destiny, actually. But remember what Mom always said. *'Show me where you've been, and I'll tell you where you're going.'* Remember?"

Amelia's bitterness only grew in reply to her sister's hard edge, so she pushed back again. "So, you think, and Mom would have thought, that I'm going to be a waitress for the rest of my life? That I'll never get a good role? That I'll never fall in love or be happy?" Anger sliced through her words. Dobi roused on her lap, curious now. She patted his head assuredly.

Kate pushed her coffee out of the way and wrapped her hand around Amelia's wrist. "No. I don't believe any of that. But I do believe you have to decide to do it. Here. Now. A new start, right? Don't slip back, Amelia. Don't move cities again. Stop searching. Start *doing*."

Amelia's chest grew hollow. Kate was right. She knew Kate was right. But the truth could be a hard pill to swallow. Amelia opened her mouth to answer but thought better of making some empty promise. Instead, she decided to *do*.

***

After a light breakfast and a jaunt down to the beach with Dobi kicking sand with feverish confusion, Amelia felt refreshed. Something about the water refilled her spirit, splashing life back into her where it had begun to drain.

Kate was hard at work in the second upstairs bath with grand plans to also finish the kitchen and start some business planning, but Amelia needed to get out of the house and set about her research project.

She kenneled Dobi with strict instructions to take a nap and, trusting that he'd do just that, took off on foot to Birch Village, the plaza of shops and eateries by the marina. There, she intended to get some basic information on the workings of lighthouses on Lake Huron. Her biggest question was *who* was now running the old Acton place? Who was in charge of the light and tending to the grounds? It would be information Michael Matuszewski, the lawyer, might have on hand, but Amelia was feeling the distinct motivation to "*do*" after all. So, while she awaited his response to her most recent text (a simple *Can we meet today?*), she strode directly to the wooden cabin at the corner of the dock and the boat ramp. If she garnered no useful details there, she intended to take Kate's SUV and drive up there herself and nose around.

The only other times Amelia had ever been to the little shack-style marina office was when she was a teenager who fooled around with cute tourists looking for boat rentals.

Otherwise, the Hannigan family had their own dock with their own boat. No need to rent a slip. Wendell had always managed their various lake vessels. When he left, Nora took over, selling everything off under the claim that she didn't have time for water sports.

Her daughters, however, had long suspected the poor woman couldn't bear to be reminded of her estranged husband.

Amelia bounced up against the serving window of the marina shack. "Hi," she greeted, flashing a toothy grin to the man inside. He was unfamiliar, but that didn't mean much. Younger, too. Handsome, undoubtedly. He reminded her a bit of her ex, Jimmy, but not enough to stir any real emotion within. Besides, Amelia was a woman on a mission. Not a girl on the prowl.

"Hiya," he answered, grinning back.

Amelia pushed her hand through her chestnut hair. "I'm looking for someone in charge," she replied coyly.

"I can be in charge," he challenged, propping his elbows on the Formica countertop in front of him and leaning forward.

Amelia grinned and glanced down then back up. "Well, I need to find out who runs the old lighthouse." She nodded over her shoulder and up the shoreline.

He looked past her and then returned his attention to Amelia. "There's a lighthouse on this lake?"

"Yeah." Amelia grimaced at his ignorance. This person was probably closer to twenty than fifty and here she was, veritably flirting with him for information like some kind of harlot.

The attendant shook his head. "I'm seasonal. Just started today, actually." He shrugged innocently then dropped his voice. "I don't even have a place to *live*, yet."

Amelia sighed. The kid's charm wore off immediately. "All right, well who's your boss? Is he around? Or *she*?"

This time, he nodded, evidently aware she was losing patience, which must have mattered to him for some reason. Perhaps Amelia seemed important. Perhaps she carried some sort of power. She straightened her back as he stood up and leaned out the window craning around it to search the dock. "There," he pointed a finger.

Amelia followed it to a second man, clad in khaki shorts, a polo and boat shoes, the men's uniform for Birch Harbor.

She nodded and thanked the boy then turned in the direction of the dock, stepping easily onto it, her blouse tickling against her skin as a fresh breeze swept past her.

"Are you the marina manager?" she asked behind him, as he finished tying off a speedboat to a piling.

He turned to face her, his expression suspicious. "Yes," he replied, his jaw set.

Amelia bristled at the cold reception. She was unused to it. "Hi," she answered. "My name is Amelia. I'm looking for some information about the lighthouse just north of town. Can you help me?"

He crossed his arms over his chest and rocked back on his feet. "What kind of information?"

Amelia searched his shirt for a name tag—anything to help gain a little traction, a little familiarity. When she saw none, she diverted the conversation away from his wariness. "My family owns the house on the harbor over on Heirloom Cove." She pointed behind him to the red house. He didn't turn. "The Hannigans," she added.

At that, he swayed again, raising his eyebrows. "Hannigan?" he replied. "I know the Hannigans."

"You do?" she frowned and cocked her head. It was Amelia's turn to be suspicious. If someone knew her family, then she ought to also know him. "I'm sorry, but how?"

His tone softened, and he dropped his hands, tucking them casually into his pockets. "I'm a transplant from Rochester," he began. She thought she detected a hint of sadness in his eyes. "I moved out here a year ago with my daughter."

Amelia felt the itch of curiosity stab her. "Then how do you know us?" she pressed.

He chuckled. "Well, I don't *know you*. I know a Hannigan, though. Miss Hannigan." The sadness drained from his face, leaving in its place a small smile.

Frowning deeper, Amelia wracked her brain. "My mom? *Nora?*"

"Nora? No, no. I know *of* Nora, though. Maybe the Miss Hannigan I know is Nora's granddaughter? She's a teacher. *Miss* Hannigan. I'm sorry, her first name escapes me, I suppose."

"Oh, Clara!" Amelia cried. "My... my *sister*, Clara."

"She's your sister?" He seemed skeptical, which Amelia did not especially appreciate. Clara wasn't *that* much younger than Amelia.

"Yes, she's my sister." Amelia was about to ask him if he worked for the school—if that was how he knew Clara, but then, there he was, tying off rentals like he owned the marina.

He shifted his weight. "My daughter has Miss Hannigan for her English class. I, um," If Amelia didn't know any better, she'd say the man was blushing.

"Right, she teaches junior high English. Her name is Clara." Amelia's frown vanished.

"Clara. Right." He seemed to mull the name over. "My daughter adores her."

At that, Amelia melted a little. Her former enthusiasm crept back into place. "That's nice to hear. My sister loves her job."

A pause formed between them, reminding Amelia what she was there for. "So," she went on, finding her rhythm again, "the lighthouse. I'm wondering if you know who runs it."

"No one," he replied, gesturing to follow her down along the dock. Almost every slip held a vessel. A gentle current rocked them about their berths. Amelia shielded her eyes from the distant sun. Ahead of her, the man pulled down a pair of Ray Bans. He looked every bit the part of a self-assured summer tourist. And yet he wasn't. He was a dad from the suburbs who managed the marina. She wondered how he stumbled across such a position. Running the Birch Harbor marina was no seasonal gig. It usually belonged to a local, someone with a good amount of prestige and a good-old-boy reputation. Not an inlander.

He grabbed a broom that had been leaning precariously against a piling and swept small puddles here and there along the deck.

"Well, what do you mean no one runs it?" she asked, following him as she studied a small rowboat that decidedly did not belong amongst the Bayliners and Yamahas.

"Technology," Jake replied, nodding behind her to indicate he was ready to head back off the dock. "Boats don't rely on lighthouses as much as they used to. And this harbor isn't big enough to warrant a payday for a lightkeeper."

Amelia's shoulders slumped forward as she followed him back to land. "Do you know anything about the last one?"

Jake propped the broom against the office and called a hello to the attendant before turning back to her. "Last what?" he asked.

"The last lightkeeper."

"Oh, right." He pushed his sunglasses back into his dark thatch of hair and crossed his arms over his chest again. "I'm sorry, but no. Like I said, I'm sort of new here. You could ask a local, though? Seems like everybody knows everybody else's business around here."

She narrowed her eyes, heat from the rising sun at her back, boiling her blood. "I *am* a local," she spat back then shook her head quickly.

"Sorry. I just... never mind. Thank you for your help, *Jake*." She offered the best smile she could muster, forcing herself to remember that her sister had to deal with this guy.

He didn't seem to notice her irritation and bid her goodbye with a warm expression. "Oh, ma'am?" he added as Amelia pushed off up the path toward Heirloom Cove.

"Your sister is a great teacher."

A little laugh caught in Amelia's throat. It was an odd addition to their otherwise stilted conversation. She waved and thanked him, knowing full-well that Clara was a good teacher.

She didn't need a marina manager newbie to tell her about her own family.

Amelia was going to find out for herself.

***

"I'm going to drive up to the lighthouse," Amelia called to Kate, wherever she was in the house.

Kate appeared in the doorframe of the kitchen. "What?"

"I'm driving up to the lighthouse."

"What about your meeting with Michael?" Kate asked, blowing a strand of blonde hair out of her eye.

"I'll call him on the way."

"He won't let you go there. Not without a key or something," Kate protested.

"It's ours, right? I don't need a key. I'll break in."

"Amelia, don't. You can't just roll back into town and make trouble. Give me an hour, and I'll come."

"I'm not waiting an hour," Amelia answered, grabbing her purse off the table by the door. "Come now if you want. I'm taking your car." She grabbed Kate's keys from the ceramic bowl on the table.

Kate propped her yellow-gloved hands on her hips and shook her head. "I can't right now. If you aren't going to wait for me, at least come back here soon and pick me up. I don't want to miss out, you know."

Amelia shook her head. "You're not missing out. I promise. If I see anything, I'll call you right away."

Kate frowned, caught between her dedication to her chores and her curiosity. She held her palms up, helpless. "Just, at least call Michael first, okay? Don't you have a meeting with him?"

Amelia opened the door and called over her shoulder, "He can meet me at the lighthouse!" before pulling it shut and striding, for the first time in a long time, with a purpose.

***

Before pulling out of the driveway, she checked her phone to find a missed text message.

Walking back from the marina was nothing short of a feat in the emerging morning heat as she had silently drawn up a mental list of who, what, when, where, and how to access the lighthouse. Her interest in the place had grown like a fever. It was the last note their mother had left them.

The lighthouse was the sisters', and Amelia agreed to take it on as her new project. Clara, entirely disinterested in the goings on of Nora's estate, was no help.

Megan, too distracted by her personal life to offer much more than excuses for why she couldn't make it to town, was useless.

And then Kate, the one sister Amelia could always count on, would rather scrub a toilet than search an abandoned lighthouse.

Sometimes, Amelia wondered if *she* was the adopted one.

But then she remembered Michael, the lawyer. Trusty, Type-A Michael. Her exact opposite, with his mahogany-and-leather office and neatly organized files and binders and his precisely knotted tie.

Perhaps he didn't much care about the lighthouse. But his interest was piqued. There was something there, at that last meeting when he rounded them up to share Nora's missing notes. He wanted to help Amelia, sure. But it was more than that. If Amelia didn't know better, she'd take him for a voyeur. After all, Michael hadn't grown up in Birch Harbor. He'd simply moved into town, sliding into his ancestral office space, taking up the work of his father and his father's father there, in *her* community.

What is it with these men who just up and moved to the lake? Amelia thought to herself as she slid a finger across her phone screen and opened the text.

It *was* from him. A long-winded reply to her inquiry. Yes, he was available. No appointments until the afternoon. Just paperwork and phone calls. She'd be a welcome break for him.

Welcome.

Amelia's gaze lingered on the last sentence before she tapped his name and put a call through.

A text would not do. She had to speak to him personally.

He answered on the first ring. "This is Michael."

"Michael, hi. It's, um, Amelia." She felt silly and wondered if he'd saved her as a contact. Maybe not.

"Yes, I know. Hi." His voice was different on the phone than in person. Warmer. Then again, maybe the phone had nothing to do with it. "Did you get my text?"

"I did, thank you," Amelia replied. "I know we were going to discuss how to... *proceed* with researching whether the Actons ever sold the lighthouse or if anyone else has a claim to it," she went on, "but I'm, well, I'm heading up there now."

"To my office?"

"No, I'm driving to the lighthouse, actually." Amelia forced a small laugh, realizing she sounded anxious and ridiculous. Maybe she *should* go to his office first. That'd be more sensible. But was Amelia ever sensible? No.

"Great idea," he replied. Amelia nearly veered off the road.

"Really?" she asked.

"Yes, we can see if someone lives there then come back and dig up any available records."

She leaned back in her seat, easing up on the gas as she drifted past Birch Village and farther north. "Oh, great. That's great." She faltered, glancing in her rear-view mirror and briefly assessing her hair. "Does this mean you'll meet me there?"

Amelia heard the grin in his voice. A man of adventure, to be sure. "I'm on my way."

Chapter 10—Kate

Kate tugged the stopper from the kitchen sink. Murky gray water swirled down the drain, gurgling on its way. She turned on the faucet and rinsed the foamy residue of the cleaning solution. Little bits of dirt and muck ran down the sides. She wiped the inner rims, her rubber gloves squeaking on the clean porcelain.

Irritated that Amelia didn't wait for her but still had the gall to take Kate's SUV, she let out a deep sigh and considered her next plan of action. There was no point walking to the lighthouse. It was too far. Clara was at work, busy and unavailable. Megan had returned home so Sarah could finish her last week of school before summer. Amelia was on a mission, fool's or otherwise.

Kate was alone in Birch Harbor. Save, perhaps, for one other individual who might be available should Kate have an emergency. Her mind flicked to Matt Fiorillo. Maybe it was a good time to call him and set something up. He could come assess her needs—the needs of the Inn, of course. Maybe he'd know someone who might want the job.

She reached into her back pocket for her phone, but it wasn't there. Retracing her steps in her head, she jogged upstairs and searched the second bath, taking a moment to admire how clean and pretty it now stood.

But there was no phone.

Kate left the bathroom and went into her bedroom, searching the bed and the nightstand then the dresser but still coming up empty.

Wracking her brain, she jogged down the wooden staircase and moved into the kitchen, but it wasn't there either. Not on the island or the table or on the counter by the fridge.

After taking a long sip from her iced tea, a lightbulb flipped on in her brain. The basket of rags. She'd taken her basket of rags down to the washing machine.

With a snap of her fingers, Kate passed through the basement door and trotted down the steps.

The basement had long been used as storage for Nora Hannigan and her daughters, but the storage was chaotic and haphazard. A mishmash of cardboard boxes and wooden crates were stuffed together along hodgepodge shelving units, lining every wall of the unfinished space. Old appliances and furniture towered at odd angles in the darkened corners. Mysterious stains spread from beneath the shelves, crawling toward each other in the center of the concrete floor.

Behind the washer and dryer, three narrow wooden racks held dusty shoeboxes. And that was where Kate had left her phone, teetering between two of the rectangular boxes just above the crack that divided the washer from the dryer. She eyed it immediately and reached for the darn thing, but as she did, Kate tripped over her basket of wet rags and tumbled right into the washing machine. The shelf behind it, where her phone sat, rattled against her fall and her phone slid straight off and knocked its way down behind the machine but got stuck.

"*No!*" Kate hissed under her breath. With a deep sigh, she briefly considered leaving the darn thing there indefinitely and getting back to work. Instead, though, she gripped the sides of the machine and pulled hard, freeing it from its rust-encrusted moorings.

The phone bounced down farther and clattered to the concrete. Kate went to the far side of the machine and reached her hand behind it, barely able to get a finger to the slender device which had wedged just under the back corner of the dryer.

Using the pad of her middle finger, she found purchase and pulled the phone inch by inch until she could grab it in victory and briefly assess that it was free of damage, before standing straight up and hitting her head on the underside of the shelf that ran along the top of the two machines.

"*Ouch,*" she groaned in time to see that the shelf was not nailed or screwed down but rather just a freely sitting plank on two brackets, and she had dislodged it from its delicate position entirely. In slow motion, the splintery wood crashed forward, spilling no fewer than four shoe-boxes and all their contents.

Heavy papers and raw-edged envelopes flopped out between every crack and crevice. Another box let loose a thick stack of yellowed doilies. And another of the boxes must have contained extra hardware for the machines. Bolts and washers and random other pieces of metal clanked along between the washer and dryer, then scattered around like a set of marbles splayed onto the floor.

Kate didn't have time for the mess. A headache immediately swelled in the base of her skull, and she shook her head unhappily. Her motivation to call Matt dissipated like a sandcastle in a rainstorm. Although, now she felt the need for help more than ever.

After tucking her phone snugly in her back pocket, she bent and grabbed the first box, intent on making a quick go of cleaning the mess and moving on. She knocked the cardboard against the wall, and dust rained down around her hand. The ache in the back of her head climbed around to her temples, and she forced it down, scooping a packet of papers from the ground and shoving them back in the box until she'd filled it to the brim.

She set the box on top of the washer and moved on to the next, knocking the dusty years from that one then plopping the doilies back inside.

Two more boxes later, she'd recovered everything that was in plain sight. The hardware that had rolled beneath the dryer would have to wait.

Now, having tended to what felt like an insurmountable setback, Kate's stomach growled to life. Suddenly aware of how starved she was, she left the basement and ascended the stairs, all four boxes piled on her forearms. Kate wasn't the sort to put off clutter. She'd rather tackle it head on, even if she had to get messy.

Once in the kitchen with the boxes neatly stacked on the center of the island, she washed her hands and then poured herself a bowl of cereal and sat on a barstool at the island, finally sliding her phone from her pocket and opening Matt's contact information.

Her thumb smeared circles around his name until she finally worked up enough confidence to send him a text.

Keeping her tone tight and her message brief, Kate simply asked if he'd be available to chat anytime soon. She had a question.

As soon as she hit send, she realized that her vaguery might have added unnecessary weight to the text and immediately tapped a second, clearer message. *I have a question about the house. It's about some repairs. That's all.*

She deleted several words then typed them again, but before she could send the second message, he replied.

Sure. Can you talk now?

Her heart dipped into her stomach and bounced back up into her throat. The skin on her neck grew hot and her back grew itchy.

"*Okay,*" she murmured to herself, digging deep for the willpower to answer. Instead of texting back, she swallowed the lump in her throat and hit the call icon.

He answered right away. "Kate, hi."

"Hi, Matt. Sorry for being a little vague," she began awkwardly. After a brief pause, she pushed ahead, reminding him of her grand plans to resuscitate the house and open a bed-and-breakfast.

"I'm happy for you, Kate. And I'm happy you're back in town, honestly."

She glowed at his reply, finding the wherewithal to hit him with her question. "Thanks, Matt. That means a lot to me." She cleared her throat. "So the reason I called is that we have some major repairs. We're looking for painters. Someone to work on the AC unit. Some plumbing issues and other things like that—"

"Sure," he cut in before she could finish. "I'm happy to help."

"Oh, no. No, no," she rushed to answer. "I didn't want to pressure you into helping me or anything. I just figured you would know some people."

"Know some people? I *am* the person," he replied with a chuckle. "I can come over whenever you're ready, Kate. Just say the word."

It was like magic. His offer thrilled her and confused her. Matt was ready and able to offer assistance, but she wasn't quite sold. Would it be a conflict of interest? Would they get along?

She thanked him and they ended their call after an agreement that he'd swing by as soon as he could.

The whole matter reminded Kate that she had some unfinished business to attend to. Namely, her old life. The one on Apple Tree Hill.

On a whim, she navigated back into her contacts and found her boss at the realty company. Kate wasn't one to rush decisions, unless, of course, she was certain.

And now, with Matt's kind offer and with half the house ready for business, she was *certain*.

Chapter 11—Clara

The last week before summer vacation was a veritable nightmare. Each day, Clara was battling more and more disruptions to her class. It didn't help that other teachers were showing movies and hosting parties whereas Clara had continued on with business as usual.

Her severe regime endeared her to only a few of her eighth graders. Most of them coped with the suffocation by asking to use the bathroom or get a drink no fewer than three times per class period.

By the end of the school day on Monday, Clara had neared the end of her resolve, and she went as far as to promise her fifth period class that they could play games the next day. Once the last hour began, Clara's planning period, she finally had a chance to breathe. A stack of essays stood menacingly on the corner of her desk. Instead of tearing into them with her red pen, she opted to take a walk to the front office and grab a box of tissues from the supply closet. It was as good an excuse as any, and she could use a little warm up. After school, she'd promised herself that she'd get a little packing done at her apartment. Then, after *that*, she told Kate she'd spend an hour in the basement with her. Clara and her sisters had so much to do, but Clara had tried to impress upon them that they had all the time in the world to do it.

She'd just as soon work bit by bit on her own move. But Clara loved her sisters and her commitment to help them was pure.

Her sensible clogs echoed softly against the hardwood floors as she walked through quiet lockers toward the office.

Once there, she slipped in through the hall door, greeting the secretary politely before stealing away into the modest closet where teachers could find extra paper, boxes of tissues, and—sometimes, if they were lucky, packages of dry erase markers.

As she rummaged through the closet, Clara heard the secretary buzz in a visitor through the front door of the school building. The visitor and his deep voice joined the secretary in a conversation. Just as

Clara had rummaged through the end-of-the-year dregs of supplies, she heard her name.

"Miss Hannigan is right here, actually!"

Clara popped her head out and glanced toward the reception desk. Standing on the other side was a familiar-looking man.

She winced. "Oh my goodness, *Mr. Hennings!*" Recovering quickly, Clara didn't reveal that she'd completely and utterly forgotten about the last-minute conference she'd scheduled with Mercy's dad. "I'm so glad to see you. Let's head back to my classroom."

Clara whirled out of the office and met him in the hall where he offered his hand to hers. She waved down the hall. "Right this way."

"Beautiful day out," he commented lightly.

Appreciating the small talk, she agreed. "Not too hot, yet. Last night I even slept with the windows open, if you can believe that." Clara cringed a little. It felt like an over-share in the presence of this veritable stranger.

But Mr. Hennings didn't falter. "This weekend's storm was a nice break. It's been a little dry."

"Are you from Birch Harbor originally?" Clara diverted the conversation as they turned the corner to her wing. She knew they weren't. Mercy had told her as much. They were from the Detroit area, probably not far from Kate's neck of the woods. Clara knew almost the entire story of why Mercy and her father left his good job at the college to come to a small tourist town.

"No. We lived outside of Detroit. I taught at Great Lakes College and ran a research lab there for marine technology and freshwater studies. We did a lot of work on Lake Huron." They paused outside Clara's door as she fumbled with her keys. She flushed under the pressure but finally inserted the right one, turned the knob and as she began to tug the door, Mr. Hennings gripped it from above her, opening it and holding it patiently as she withdrew her key and stepped in.

"What a neat job," she replied, smiling up at him. "And, thanks. We can leave this open or close it if you'd like?" Normally, Clara kept the door open during parent conferences, unless an administrator or another teacher happened to be present too. She should have just done that, prop it open. She silently cursed herself for another awkward moment.

"Oh, it doesn't matter to me. Whatever you prefer." He tucked his hands in his khaki shorts pockets and waited by the door as she dumped the boxes of tissues on a nearby student desk.

The door naturally swung shut, and Clara chose to leave it be. Not make a bigger deal. "Come sit down," she said to him, waving at a chair beside her desk.

He waited until she sat then followed her example and eased down.

Uncertain just how to begin, since their conference was the result of a flippant offer she'd made a few days before (rather than anything out of necessity), Clara swallowed and asked, "So what brought you to Birch Harbor? A research project, or...?"

Mr. Hennings glanced left then replied after an extended beat. "Just a fresh start."

Clara blinked. Maybe he didn't want to talk about it. She couldn't blame him.

"So," she answered brightly. "Mercy."

A broad grin swept across Mr. Hennings' face. He leaned forward, closer to Clara. Warmth crawled up her neck.

"Yes," he said. "First of all, thank you for suggesting the conference. I don't... I *haven't* always come to parent-teacher-type meetings. Her mother used to do that. Not that she needed to either. Mercy is more responsible than me, probably." He chuckled and rubbed his hands along his shorts.

Clara forced herself to focus on her computer screen as she navigated into her online grade book. "Well, she's *certainly* more responsible than me," she joked, laughing lightly. Then she turned serious. "Mercy is truly an exceptional young lady, Mr. Hennings."

"Thank you for saying that. I happen to agree with you, but it's nice to hear it from someone else, you know?" He hesitated and a thoughtful expression darkened his face. Clara slid her hand off her mouse and swiveled in her chair to face him. He looked up at her, a frown crinkling the skin between his eyebrows. "I worry about her sometimes."

"Mercy?" Clara fell back a little. What could he possibly worry about with Mercy? She was brilliant and kind, smart and hard-working. His comment left her to ignore for the moment just how nervous she seemed to be around him. "What are you worried about?" Clara felt her face flush as she wracked her brain for any incidents in the past couple weeks. Anything to suggest Mercy was less than thriving. She came up empty.

"New girl. New school. I know how teenagers can be, and Mercy, well," he pressed his lips into a thin line. "She's more concerned with straight A's than happiness."

Clara thought about that for a moment. "To Mercy," she began, treading on thin ice. It was never smart to cross the line between teacher and parent, especially when Clara had no children of her own. No parental experience to speak of. But she pushed ahead. "Straight A's *are* happiness." She shrugged and felt lame.

"That's no way to spend a childhood, though."

She looked up at him, meeting his gaze. For being the father of a fourteen-year-old, he lacked the middle-agedness that most of her students' parents bore. No silver hairs at the temples. No paunchy stomach. And yet, despite his evident youthfulness, he reflected the wisdom of an old soul.

Clara immediately conjured images of her own father and crossed them with each man she had ever been on a date with. It was complicated and confusing, the feelings that currently fought their way to the surface of her mind. Nonetheless, she pushed them down hard and addressed his concern.

"You wonder if Mercy fits in?"

He looked at his hands then back up at her. "Something like that. I just want her to have a good life. I want her to have close relationships. Friendships."

Clara understood exactly what he needed to hear. He needed to hear that Mercy was more than a student—that she was a joiner, too. But the problem was, she *wasn't*. Mercy was a mini Clara. Isolated, nervous, and introverted. She tried a small smile, lifting her hands. "Mr. Hennings, Mercy is a kind-hearted girl. She's a leader, academically. She might not want to be a cheerleader or join the drama club, but I think you've done a great job with her. You and her mom, I mean. Mercy is perfect just the way she is." As the words curled off her tongue, Clara realized she was saying those things to herself as much as she was to the girl's father. And, it felt good. She bit her lower lip and raised her eyebrows.

Mr. Hennings was smiling back and nodding his head. "You're right. You're right. I guess it's just what dads do. Worry, that is. Thanks for your time today, Miss Hannigan."

"Oh, please, Mr. Hennings. Call me Clara." She narrowed her gaze on him, and suddenly he seemed ten years younger. His face free of worry now, he looked more like a peer to Clara and less like a parent, less like her father.

"Clara. Oh, and you can call me Jake."

***

Somehow, one thing led to another and Clara had walked Jake clear out to the front office. The secretary gave her a knowing look, but she tried to ignore it, instead turning her focus on her after-school plans.

As soon as Clara left school and headed to her apartment, her phone rang.

She glanced at the screen. *Amelia*. Clara hit *Accept*. "Hey."

"Are you still at school?" Amelia asked, breathlessly.

"I'm just leaving. Why? Is everything okay?"

"I'm at the lighthouse with Michael."

Clara squinted through the late afternoon sun. "Michael?"

"The lawyer. Yes. We can't get in. It's locked. Kate can't find a key at the house. Can you swing by the cottage and dig around for a bit?"

Just as she was about to swing left onto the main drag, Clara flipped her turn signal in the other direction, toward where the cottage sat inland on Birch Creek. "Sure," she replied, though deep down Clara knew it was a fool's mission. She had no idea where to begin to look. It was going to take days to sort through everything in that place. "Are you *sure* it's not at the house on the harbor?" she pressed, skeptical.

"No, I'm not." A crackling sound cut across the line before Amelia came back on. "But if you could look that might help, okay?"

It felt like Clara had no choice. Her packing session had officially been derailed by Amelia's urgent need to get into the lighthouse. Impatience was distinctly a Hannigan virtue, but one that had not been passed on to Clara. "Fine," she murmured through the phone. "I'll call you if I find something." She clicked off, accelerated down the road and toward the cottage. Her future home. At least, Clara thought to herself, she enjoyed being at the cottage.

***

After walking up the cobblestone path, Clara unlocked the door to the cottage and pushed it open, stalling for a moment on the threshold. She hadn't been in the little house since just before the funeral, when she and Kate carefully selected a pretty white lace nightgown for their mother. It had been a specific request. Nora wanted to rest when it was time for her final rest. *Don't have them drape me in some ridiculous gown,* she'd said.

Clara already knew which nightdress to select. It was one Nora had purchased on vacation one year in New York. She'd never worn it, and when Clara asked her why not, she said she was saving it.

Tears threatened at the corners of her eyes and she silently cursed Amelia for making her go there alone.

Sucking a deep breath in, she walked directly to the little table by the door and slid open the drawer. Rummaging around inside proved useless. There was nothing in there except a book of matches, a flashlight, a candle, and a back-up key fob for Clara's own vehicle. Nora had gotten rid of her own car years earlier.

She shoved the drawer shut and dipped her hand into the basket on top, finding a couple of plastic-wrapped mints, Nora's late Chihuahua's collar, and a packet of bills. Clara grabbed the bills and tucked them into the crevice of the front door so as not to forget.

Then, she began to forage in the junk drawer in the kitchen. As expected, mostly junk revealed itself. Highlighters and notepads, screws and a tape measure, another flashlight, a packet of flossing sticks. As Clara began to close the drawer, it got jammed. She yanked it out and pushed again, but something was stuck in the far back. Her fingers crawled to the back of the drawer, alighting on the cause of the jam, a thick notebook.

As she drew it out, her eyes danced across its surface. It was bound in a dusty fabric and bore no indication of what might be inside.

Clara wondered if she even ought to look.

If it was her place to look.

After all, the last time a secret document surfaced, it changed *everything*.

Chapter 12—Megan

Exactly one month earlier, Megan had applied for a position with Mistletoe, a matchmaking app based out of South Carolina. From what she could tell (and assuming she landed the job) she would be able to work remotely from Michigan and simply travel down for training or conferences. It was a dream for Megan—not necessarily moving away from Michigan—but working with a matchmaking company.

When Megan had revealed her hopes about it to Amelia, she had continued to press her on *why* she couldn't seem to tear her eyes off her phone the prior week. Amelia did not act surprised that Megan had an interest in matchmaking, but she claimed she was surprised that Megan kept the application so secretive.

The truth was Megan knew what people would think. There she was an almost-divorcee about to bear the burden of an empty nest. How cliché to struggle to find something to fill her time now. And how pathetic that she'd have to start making a living on her own, without the help of her fumbling techie husband.

Plus, Megan wasn't the sort who immediately inspired someone to find his or her soulmate. Her dark wardrobe, black nails, and thick eyeliner aligned better with a mortician than a matchmaker. Still, set-ups were Megan's *thing*. They always had been. Even Brian had sometimes joined her in pairing off friends and engineering successful courtships. In fact, that's how she and Brian had met. Through a set-up; a blind date.

Megan couldn't help but revisit those early days in her mind's eye. Brian waiting awkwardly in front of the Italian restaurant just down the street from her dormitory. Their first kiss just outside her room. He didn't even ask to come in, and never would. He left so much up to Megan in those college days. She never stopped to think if he ought to have. Maybe their lives would be different. Maybe college would have panned out for her without the pressure of managing their blossoming relationship.

Yes, Megan began college.

No, she did not graduate.

Sometimes, she wondered if that was her own fault or Brian's or what. Maybe no one's. Maybe just one of those things in life that was ever and always undone. Much like her divorce was shaping up to be.

Presently, she sat at her in-home office desk. Neither she nor Brian had taken one step toward packing. They stood firmly at an impasse. And their lawyers were the only ones benefiting. Although, even the money-hungry attorneys were tired of the indecision.

A digital clock on the desk reminded Megan that Sarah would be home soon, probably giddy with excitement that summer was so near at hand. Having quit volleyball, the teenager had no plans except to get back to Birch Harbor, which Megan partially appreciated, since she'd like to be anywhere other than in a shared space with Brian Stevenson.

She clicked open a browser and navigated to her email. Having received no phone call or message from the hiring manager at Mistletoe, she was forced to access their online interface to check the status of her application. Over the past four weeks, she'd watched as her application advanced through three out of who-knew-how-many steps of the hiring process.

Week one, her application was marked as *received*.

Week two, her application was marked as *processing*.

Week three, her application was marked as *in review*. Megan didn't know the difference between *processing* and *in review*.

And last week, nothing. No progress whatsoever. She hoped to see something—*anything*—to assure her that she was good enough to be a social media manager for some small-beans dating app.

Clicking through the confirmation email to their applicant interface, Megan noticed a new note in her application status.

Rejected.

Her jaw nearly hit the desk and her face grew warm. A feverish anxiety crept beneath her blouse and her knee began bobbing in rapid succession.

Rejected.

No. No. No. It had to be an *error*.

Didn't they know who she was? She was smart and witty and had a great sense of social media management. She had a *teenager* for goodness' sake. A direct connection to the stupid app's future demographic!

She searched the page for anything else—a link to personal notes or some sort of reply, but nothing. Nothing to explain why she couldn't join the workforce like every other middle-aged, former-housewife, mid-life crisis-stricken woman. Now, she was *worse* than a cliché. She was a *reject*.

Sobs crawled up her throat and tears filled her vision as she pushed the heels of her hands hard into her eye sockets.

"Are you okay?"

The deep voice roused Megan with a start. She looked up, tears staining her cheeks, her mouth wet with spittle. "No," she sobbed to Brian, who stood helplessly in the door frame. Megan didn't even know he was home.

She pushed her hands back into her eyes and slumped onto the desk, but his footsteps drew close and—to Megan's great surprise—he rested a hand on her shoulder. Still, despite the unwanted relief that filled her heart, she didn't turn and look at him.

"Megan," he said softly. "Is it the divorce?"

At that she turned, shaking her head weepily. "Actually, no. It's not that."

His hand fell from her shoulder and he studied the computer screen. "What's this?" he asked.

Embarrassed now, she clicked out and rubbed the tears from her eyes. "Nothing. I just... I applied for a job. Didn't get it. That's all."

He raised his eyebrows at her, but she looked away out the window, wondering where Sarah was. She should be home any minute. Megan had better pull herself together and push away the disappointment. She had a daughter to be normal for.

"I'm fine, really. It's just been a hard few weeks."

"Actually," he answered, stepping back and lowering himself into the wooden chair that stood to the side of the desk.

The chair was meant to be a piece of decor, not a piece of furniture, but men didn't understand those things. In over two decades of marriage, Brian had never learned to stop drying his hands on the decorative towels. He slept on throw pillows. He often dragged a perfectly poised flannel blanket off the arm of the rocking chair and over his lap during their nightly viewings of JEOPARDY! even when there was a stack of cuddling blankets in the basket by the TV.

For a very long time, Megan found his willful ignorance somehow endearing. Like so many things, though, the habit lost its charm and turned into a pet peeve for her.

She rubbed her eyes hard, like a child, and propped an elbow on the desk, staring impatiently at him, waiting for him to lean into some lecture on how they needed to get the paperwork done.

He cleared his throat. "I'm sorry about everything, Megan." His voice had dropped lower, and his gaze was on his lap where he picked at a hangnail.

"What are you talking about?" Her disappointment over the job still clung to her heart, but his apology softened the tension in her shoulders.

He shrugged and squeezed his eyes shut. "I should have come to the funeral... I should have *insisted*."

"Are you talking about *Mom's* funeral?" She narrowed her eyes on him, a little bewildered. "I told you I didn't want you there," she replied, her voice flat and lifeless. It was the truth. Nora didn't need her daughter's marital drama in death, too.

"I should have gone. It's... Megan, it's killing me that I didn't."

Megan looked up, now entirely baffled by this sudden show of sympathy. "Why is it killing you? We're getting a divorce, Brian. It doesn't matter if you show up to my family commitments. In fact, you shouldn't anymore, if that's not obvious. That's what a divorce means. That we aren't family anymore. You know?" As the words sliced out of her mouth, a bitter taste developed on her tongue. She didn't believe a thing she was saying. She frowned and shook her head, looking away again. Megan could not face this hypocrite of a man who requested a divorce from her but now decided he wanted a piece of her life still.

His tone changed abruptly. "I'm going to Birch Harbor on Wednesday. I'm visiting your mom's gravesite. I hope that's okay with you." He rose shakily, and Megan's eyes crawled from his jeans to his shirt to his face.

"You're *what*?"

"I can't live with myself about it anymore. I'm going to say my goodbyes to her. I loved your mom. Despite... despite everything."

Megan shook her head, wincing at an oncoming headache. "Brian, we're getting a *divorce*." She didn't know how much clearer she could be.

He had turned to leave but now whipped back around, his hands tucked neatly in his pockets. "Yeah, well. We're not divorced yet." She was about to protest further but he pulled a hand out from his jeans and waved it to the door. "You and Sarah can come, too, you know." And with that, Megan's husband had the gall to smile at her. A sincere, heart-stopping *smile*.

***

"I'm coming back to town on Wednesday." Megan was on the phone with Kate. Sarah had made it home from school and was now freaking out about her parents' news that she'd be missing the last day. Megan had already tried to reassure her daughter that the *Yearbook Signing* and *Cafeteria Social* would not impact her ability to graduate the next year.

"Why *Wednesday*?" Kate asked.

Megan shook her head as she poured herself an early evening glass of wine. "Brian is going to a conference on Thursday and won't be home until Sunday."

"Wait a minute. Back up please."

Megan winced. Here it came. The Spanish inquisition. Or, rather, the Hannigan Inquisition. She cleared her throat, took a fast swig then launched into an awkward explanation of the fact that Brian was struggling with guilt about missing the funeral and wanted to pay his respects, and Megan thought it would be weird for him to go without her, and, well, they were all going together. Like one big happy family.

"Brian? As in your husband who you keep trying to convince us that you're divorcing?"

Megan felt her face flush, though it might have been from the wine. "That's the one," she replied, leaning back into her recliner as she clicked the television set on. She didn't want to talk to Kate. She wanted to talk to Amelia, with whom she could share news about her job rejection. Plus, Amelia was always more sympathetic than Kate, who often took the position of critical mother more than empathizing sister.

"That's great," Kate said, her voice bright.

Megan frowned. "It is?"

"Of course it is. I was surprised he didn't come to the funeral to begin with."

"I told him not to, and he listened for once in our marriage." Megan bristled under the judgment. Despite their inevitable dissolution, she felt she had to defend the guy. How humiliating. "He wouldn't have anyway," she added as an afterthought.

"Yes, he would have. Brian isn't one to miss family functions."

"Well, we're not family anymore," Megan reasoned, although her voice was growing wobbly.

"Whatever," Kate shot back.

Megan felt hurt at her sister's edgy reply and heaved herself back into an upright position. "Well, anyway, we probably won't stay the night. Just drive down and back. I'm not even sure why I told you, except I might not make it to town this weekend."

"Why not?" Kate pressed.

Megan let out an exaggerated sigh. "If I have to drive down tomorrow, then I probably won't feel like driving down again in two days."

"Megan, we have a lot to do here."

Kate's voice was full of guilt, something Megan was particularly experienced with. Even so, Megan had bluffed. She would return for the weekend. After all, she had nothing better to do, especially now that she had no job offer. A distraction would be useful. "All right," she replied at length, setting her wine glass down and flipping blindly through channels.

"So, you're coming this weekend, too?"

"Yeah," Megan answered. An idea surged in her head, but the logistics would be tricky. "Maybe I'll even leave Sarah there for the rest of the week, actually. She'd love to help, and she'll be done with school since Wednesday would have been her last day of the semester."

"Sounds great to me." Kate's voice lifted at the offer of help, and Megan couldn't help but wonder if her oldest sister was on the verge of turning into Nora.

"Maybe we can meet for a late lunch after we go to the cemetery. How does Fiorillo's sound? One o'clock?"

Kate hesitated a moment before replying, "I already have lunch plans tomorrow, actually..."

Megan's interest caught on a particularly mind-numbing reality show. "Plans? What, with Amelia or something?"

"No," Kate answered. "With, um, Matt. Matt Fiorillo."

A cackle slipped out of Megan's mouth; she couldn't contain it. She apologized quickly then slapped a hand on her thigh. "You know what, Kate? Why don't we just make it a double date then?"

Chapter 13—Amelia

Amelia had just finished a third phone call with Kate after a second phone call with Clara. Both had come up empty in response to Amelia's request. No key. Nowhere. No how.

Now she stood outside of the lighthouse with Michael but with no way to enter the premises. Were it just Amelia there, she'd take a rock, pop it through the window in the door, reach in, expertly unlock said door, open, enter, and explore.

All that proved impossible in the presence of a serious-minded attorney. Amelia shoved her phone into her boho bag and crossed her arms, studying both the lighthouse and Michael in turn. Somehow the two *went* together. White paint chipped off at the corners and along the seams where the walls met the windows and the door met its frame. A square, modest house, really, its height stood no chance against the stone tower. Still, it carried a charm and charisma that wasn't necessarily an effect of its situation. It could be a sweet little house all its own.

Michael, for his part, also presented something of a duality. His good looks and evidently single status didn't quite go together. But, beneath the surface was no charming ladies' man. Instead, he was serious and earnest. And maybe, Amelia thought, rather cautious.

She wondered, briefly, what it was like to be a fearful person and if it wasn't a quality she'd do well to embrace at times. *Okay*, maybe not *fearfulness*... but, well *rather cautious*. Too often in Amelia's life she'd acted recklessly, hiding behind her impulses instead of taming them. She identified as free-spirited, bohemian, and creative but in reality, was little more than a directionless dreamer.

Amelia bit down on her lip and squinted as she began trekking back toward the house—and Michael.

"Let's do another loop," she suggested to him once they met back up. They'd already circled the lighthouse twice, looking for a point of egress, which Michael still felt uncomfortable about.

He cleared his throat and crossed his arms over his chest. "All right. After that, we can jump online and search the Registry of Deeds or, if you'd rather, head into the County Assessor. *Someone* is paying taxes on this place. It's not totally abandoned."

She nodded then took off along the house and toward the tower, or whatever it was called. Amelia figured now was as good a time as any to learn about lighthouses. Growing up, the one in Birch Harbor should have been more relevant to her. After all, her grandparents had lived there, and it was the same place her father grew up.

The truth was, however, that Amelia and her sisters had little to do with the Actons. Nora and Wendell, for the years they were still together, always hosted family events. The few times the girls had visited their grandparents in the creaky old lighthouse, they were not allowed to play anywhere near the tower. Instead, they were relegated to their father's old toys—rusty metal Tonka Trucks and shovels and pails on the modest stretch of beach that technically belonged to the county.

Amelia recalled one summer when Megan was splashing in the water—she must have been around seven or eight—and a boat sped close to the shoreline, sending up a heaving wave that toppled Amelia's little sister face first into the water. She'd come up choking and sputtering, panicked. Grandma Acton didn't even stop washing the dishes when Kate sent Amelia in to report the news. The old woman wasn't too concerned—she'd never been as warm and nurturing a grandmother as the girls might have liked. Austere, old, and always concerned over money: those were Grandma Acton's attributes.

Kate, on the other hand, tended carefully to Megan, forcing her to cough and blow her nose into Kate's ratty beach towel.

Amelia recalled watching with interest at how well Kate handled the emergency. Now, for the first time, it dawned on her how dangerous it could be for young children to play in the water with no supervision.

"Mom's estate," she mused, as she ran a hand along the chipping brick tower. She turned to catch Michael's reaction.

"You mean you think your mom's estate covers the taxes? It wasn't in her paperwork, though." He scratched his head.

"Hmm," she replied, frowning. "If not her, then who?"

Michael shrugged. "It'll be easy to figure out once we sit down to it."

Nodding, she had reached the lake side of the property. Only a few yards of sand broke the distance between where they stood together and the dock belonging to the lighthouse.

"What happened when your dad's folks passed?" Michael asked, his voice nearly fading away on a light breeze that crossed up from the lake.

Amelia shrugged. "We weren't close to them. Before they passed, they moved together into an assisted living facility in Detroit. They didn't have other children than our father, but they did have younger siblings and relatives they were closer to. When Grandpa and Grandma Acton passed, we were in our twenties. Megan had just met Brian, I think. She didn't go to the funeral. I remember that very clearly because she was close enough to go, but it was... I'm not sure. It was an uncomfortable thing, for some reason. I was living in California at the time. You know, I think Kate and Clara went. We could ask them," she suggested.

He seemed to consider what she said for a moment, adding only a quiet utterance as if he understood. She supposed he probably did. After all, didn't attorneys see the worst of humanity? She was quite confident the Hannigans weren't the worst.

They strode side by side to the dock, and Amelia studied it carefully. During its use, the Actons had their own vessels tied up there—a modest rowboat which Grandpa Acton had called his greatest weapon in times of stress (Amelia never understood that as a child, and even now she wasn't quite sure). He also had a Coastguard issued speedboat which he used to provide maintenance on the buoys and other navigational tools that existed away from the lighthouse. A thought occurred to her as she took note of the barren dock that seemed precarious enough to detach and sink directly into Lake Huron.

"He didn't even own his own speed boat here," she said as much to herself as she did to Michael.

His head whipped up to her. "That's right," he said, snapping his fingers and pointing up at the tower.

She went on, "I don't know if the Actons *actually* owned this place."

The thought horrified her for a few reasons. One, it was sad to think her grandparents didn't have something that belonged to them. Two, it meant that Nora's diary entry was either a mistake or a lie. Amelia scrounged her memory for the date of the entry, wondering if the poor woman had committed the information to paper in the throes of her illness. And lastly, if the Actons didn't own the lighthouse, then neither could Amelia nor her sisters.

Her final thought was novel—a complaint Amelia didn't even realize she would have. After all, why would she *want* the lighthouse? She didn't. She wouldn't. What she wanted was a great role in a great town—or city—and some snazzy condo where she could host functions every weekend. Maybe it'd have a little yard for Dobi. Those were her dreams.

Not a lighthouse on the lake.

"Hey," Michael said, interrupting her reverie. Amelia shook her head, her frown lifting as she smiled at him, now confident in her decision to let go and let God. Whatever became of the place was out of her control.

"Yeah?" she answered, walking nearer to his position at the corner where the dock met the lake and shore.

"Look." He pointed a couple of yards offshore along the dock.

Amelia squinted but shook her head. "What am I looking at?"

He raised his eyebrows at her, his expression unreadable, then turned in the sand and crossed in front of her and onto the dock, walking steadily.

"I wouldn't walk on that," she pointed out but followed him, anyway.

He strode a few paces across the worn boards then knelt by a piling and reached beneath the dock.

Amelia crossed her arms and studied him with suspicion.

After wiggling his hand around for some moments, he broke it free and revealed a mud-encrusted wristwatch. He held it up, and the sun glinted off its waterlogged face. Amelia did not recognize it immediately. After all, all men wore watches like that—and anyway, it was nearly a relic, like something recovered from a shipwreck.

Still, her stomach churned, and when Amelia met Michael's gaze, it was clear they shared the same thought.

Chapter 14—Kate

Matt was enthusiastic about assessing the house. So much so that he said he'd be over in the afternoon. This both thrilled and scared Kate. Mostly thrilled her. There was nothing wrong with reconnecting with one's old friend, or flame for that matter, right?

After all, enough time had passed since Paul's death. The kids were out of the house. More or less. Only two little things kept Kate from entirely immersing herself in Birch Harbor and the burgeoning Heirloom Inn: her job and her house.

Sitting there at the kitchen island, shoeboxes of the past tempting her to dig in and a fresh vase of flowers glowing nearby, a new beginning called to her. So much so that Kate picked her phone back up and made the call of a lifetime, the call that would push her to commit full time to this new phase of life.

First, when her boss answered, she told him to drop the price on her house as low as possible. Next, she quit.

As she clicked off the call, Kate's hands trembled. Just two weeks earlier, her life was in veritable shambles. Her mother had died. The will was a mess of confusion. And the truth about Kate and Clara threatened to change everything.

Now, that truth *had* changed everything. It allowed Kate to fulfill a role she'd often longed for. And, the truth and the aftermath of Nora's death allowed Kate to come home and stay there. Yes, sadness lingered. It always would no matter where Kate threw down a fresh set of roots. But at least she was near Clara. And even Amelia was home, too. Kate felt the burning sensation that would well in the pit of her stomach just before a family vacation when she was a girl.

One summer, her father and mother took them on a cross-country road trip. Destination? Nowhere. It was all about the journey, Wendell Acton had declared. Kate recalled that their mother wasn't quite on board with such a venture. Nora was more the type to execute as strict a trip as possible, preferring air travel and lux hotels over long drives and camping.

The funny thing was, Nora was not a product of moneyed folks. Quite the opposite. Though the Hannigans were some of the earliest settlers to the area, they were known for their gritty work ethic and down-home values far more than flashy lifestyles.

Sometimes, it seemed to Kate that Nora was trying to run from something. A past of hard work? No. Nora worked as hard as her parents or harder. A past of heartache? Kate didn't think so. As far as she could tell her mother worked hard, found love, played hard. End of story. But Kate wasn't blind to the laws of humanity. For every peculiarity that existed in a person's constitution, there also existed a cause.

That particular summer, when Nora surprised them all and agreed to go along on a tour of the States, as Wendell began calling it, Kate, Amelia, and Megan bubbled with excitement, dragging pillows and blankets into the backseat of the Volkswagen. Kate had helped her mother in filling two coolers with drinks and snacks and laying out as much of an itinerary as they could manage under the strict orders from their father that they simply "see where the road would take them."

The trip wove dutifully through various landmarks, and the girls enjoyed visiting such prominent sites as New York City and all it had to offer, Washington D.C. and its inspiring history, Mount Rushmore, Yosemite, Yellowstone, and even the Grand Canyon. By the time they'd returned home, Nora and Wendell were as reconnected as a married couple could be. Inspired to make the trip again in the future, Kate wondered if her life would change and her parents would get along for good.

But their arguments continued. Wendell's preference for the simple life and interest in preservation was no match for Nora's desperation to be something more than who she was. Their love story may have begun from a passionate (albeit arranged) courtship, but there always seemed to be an underlying current of conflict that drove them into frequent arguments which Kate wished to escape.

"Kate!"

Amelia's voice screeched through the front door. Kate stood from the kitchen island and rushed to the hall, certain she was about to find an emergency on her doorstep.

But it was Amelia, windblown and thrusting some object out ahead of her. Behind Amelia came Michael, also windblown, looking equally feverish and excited.

"What is it?" Kate squinted as they crossed to each other and met along the staircase.

Amelia answered, "Look what we found!"

Kate opened her hands, and her sister delicately placed a corroded, rust-riddled wristwatch in her hand. She turned it over, careful to avoid scratching her skin. The accessory was in bad condition.

"Turn it over again. Look at the back," Amelia prompted with glee.

Kate did turn it and drew the thing closer to her face. There was clearly some script on the backside, but without her readers, Kate couldn't make it out to save her life. "What does it say?" she asked.

Amelia snatched it back and held it up to her face, though Kate had the feeling that whatever was inscribed on the back of the watch had already been committed to her sister's memory. The younger of the two read aloud without any flourish. "For W. Love N."

***

Now, they sat around the kitchen table—Kate, Amelia, and Michael. A fresh pitcher of iced tea sat untouched in the center next to a hastily prepped charcuterie board, leftovers of this and that jumbled together as a makeshift appetizer.

Matt was going to join them, too. Kate had half a mind to cancel on him. Partly, she preferred they meet alone. Then again, she hated to change his plans on him.

Now, Kate and Amelia were wondering back and forth whether they ought to drag Clara over to share in the discovery. They'd already called Megan, who'd received the news with vague interest.

"May I interject?" Michael asked politely. Kate watched as Amelia flicked an urgent glance to him. He looked back at her and they shared a small smile. Kate wondered what else happened while they were out at the lighthouse digging around in the sand.

Since Amelia was too distracted by whatever daydream she was enjoying, Kate answered for the both of them. "Of course, Michael. Go ahead."

"Regardless of who you want to inform, it seems there are a couple of notable details."

Kate nodded and looked at Amelia, who simply stared at the lawyer.

He went on. "The first thing concerns your mother's note about the lighthouse and its ownership. Amelia thought that perhaps the lighthouse still belongs to the county or even the Coast Guard." He dipped his chin at her as if to pass along some validation.

Kate raised her eyebrows. "Oh my. I never thought of that. I mean, I haven't thought much about the place at all, but... *wow*. Why would our mother write that it would be ours, then?"

He shrugged his shoulders, shedding some of the authority he naturally emitted. "Maybe she didn't know but thought to mention it."

"Why didn't she say something while she was still alive?" Amelia snapped out of her daze, her expression growing edgy. She frowned at Kate, who wondered the same thing.

Nodding, Kate answered helplessly, "I don't know. I think her confusion was part of the problem. It's like there was a battle going on inside her—a will to maintain her power and control from the grave and the fight of the good person who lived deeper inside." Kate swallowed, pushing down a wave of tears. "The one who wanted her daughters to have the world."

Amelia reached across the table and grabbed her sister's hand, squeezing and smiling sadly. "Mom always wanted the best for us, Kate."

Blinking away pesky tears, Kate nodded. "You're right." But something didn't sit well. Her mother's secret diary, its difficult revelations, and now a trinket from their father? More than a trinket actually... "Wait a minute. Stay right here." Kate rose abruptly and jogged upstairs to her bedroom, plucking her reading glasses from her nightstand and jogging back downstairs.

She slid them on as she approached the table and put her hand out. "Can I see that?" Amelia passed the watch back to Kate who studied it carefully.

After some moments, she finally shared her findings. "This is the watch that Mom left you in the will, right?"

Amelia shrugged. "Yes, I assume so, I guess?"

Kate shook her head. "Why would mom include it if it was out by the lake all these years?"

Frowning, Amelia glanced to Michael for an answer, but he had none.

"Maybe," Kate mused, tapping a finger on her chin and narrowing her eyes on the watch again, "she knew it was missing. Maybe Mom wanted us to find it."

***

The doorbell rang.

Kate stood and strode to it, leaving Michael and Amelia on the laptop to conduct a property search and get underway with their new investigation. Kate was growing more and more interested in the mystery of the lighthouse and their father's timepiece, but she was equally excited to see Matt and talk about the Inn. Her growing list of projects and a newfound energy must have washed ten years from her face, because when she opened the door, clad in worn jeans, a flannel, and a makeup-free face, Matt looked... surprised.

"Kate," he gasped as she opened the door.

Kate flushed, and a broad smile drew her face up in delight at his reaction. "Hi." A small giggle escaped her lips, and he laughed too.

"I'm sorry. I just. You look great." He tried to hide his emotions by taking a step back and pretending to examine the exterior siding on the porch. Kate smiled.

"Come on in. We've been a little sidetracked in here."

"*We*?" he asked. If she didn't know better, Kate would have thought there was a hint of disappointment in his voice.

"Amelia is here with, um, Michael Matuszewski. Do you know him? He handled our mother's estate."

"Yeah, I know Michael," Matt answered. "I had to work with him on some litigation about one of our flips, actually."

Kate stared hard at Matt, waiting for him to report that Michael was too much of a lawyer for his blood, or some sort of comment one might expect from a blue-collar type like Matt. But he didn't say anything. Instead, he dipped his chin at her and frowned. "Is everything okay?"

"Oh," Kate answered lightly. "Yes, yes. I'm sorry, I wasn't clear. He and Amelia have sort of... um... *teamed up* to chase down some information about our father. It's—" she blinked and pressed a hand to her face in slight embarrassment at what must have looked like compounding family drama. "It's nothing serious. They just stopped by. Please, Matt, come in." She stepped aside and waved a hand in. He grinned, nodded his head, and stepped in, taking in the house as if he was seeing it for the first time. Of course, he wasn't, but he certainly put on a good show. Kate wondered if he was trying a little too hard to play along.

There was no game afoot, however. She really did need help with the house. It just so happened that her high school sweetheart was the right man for the job, despite their complicated history.

"Matt, hi!" Amelia beamed from the kitchen as Kate showed him in.

Michael rose from the table and greeted Matt with a handshake. Kate was reminded of how small a town Birch Harbor was, and it filled her chest with warmth.

"Matt is going to help me find someone to tackle a few projects around here," Kate began to explain.

Michael cleared his throat. "What, is Matt booked?"

Heat rushed to Kate's face, and she shot daggers at Michael who shrank back and raised his hands in self-defense. She shook her head and blinked, unsure how to respond.

For his part, Matt grinned. "I may be booked, but if Kate would have me, I'd love to work on this place." He ran a hand over his mouth and cocked his head back, staring up at the exposed beams.

Michael and Amelia excused themselves, Amelia whispering to Kate that they'd come up with a game plan regarding the watch, which Kate had almost entirely forgotten about.

Their absence and Kate and Matt's newfound privacy made her skin prickle to life. Matt had been to the house a few times in the last couple weeks. Before she and her sisters unofficially named it the Heirloom Inn, he'd shown up inquiring about its fate. Kate recalled that conversation now, replaying his justification over and again.

"Matt," she said, her voice catching in her throat. She cleared it and repeated herself. "Matt."

He'd been running his hand along the chair rail that wrapped the breakfast nook. "Yeah?" Licking his lips, Matt retrieved his hand, tucking it into his pocket before giving Kate his full attention. "Kate?" he asked, his eyes shining against the backdrop of the lake through the windows. Kate wondered if it wasn't the most beautiful view she'd ever enjoyed.

She swallowed and went on. "You said before that you wanted to make sure the house wasn't sold off. That you were concerned over

Clara, right? You wanted to make sure that between the two of us, Clara would have something." They locked eyes, and when the name fell from Kate's lips, Matt's expression darkened. Maybe this wasn't the time for such a conversation. She squeezed her eyes shut and shook her head, raising her hand to her temple in regret.

"Right," he answered quietly. "But I didn't *know* anything," he added quickly.

"What do you mean?"

"I mean I didn't know your mom never officially adopted her. I didn't know she'd be left out of the will."

"Then why were you concerned about it?" An accusatory tone rose in Kate's voice, but she didn't mean to make an issue of it. She was genuinely curious. She took a deep breath and lowered herself into a seat at the table, gesturing for him to follow.

Sitting, Matt copied her, inhaling and exhaling deeply. "After you'd left for college, I came back here. I guess I regretted our decision." He looked away, out the window, one hand rubbing the back of his neck.

"You regretted allowing my mom to raise Clara?"

"No. Well... *yes*. I regretted that we didn't make a go of it. You know?"

She conjured the nerve to reach across the table and cover his hand in hers. "Matt," Kate whispered. "I'm so sorry."

He jolted a little beneath her touch then met her gaze. "Sorry for what? It was the best decision... I just mean—"

"No, I agree. What would we have done with a baby? Live in a motel room?" She laughed, but it fell away fast. "I mean I can't imagine how hard it was for you to stay in town and not be near her. Clara, I mean. You didn't get a chance. At least I was here. I had access. You had... *nothing*." Kate's voice broke on the last word. A deep pit of sorrow opened in her chest and from it tears crawled up her throat, constricting it like a kinked hose.

Matt rubbed his eyes with his free hand then turned the other over, opening his palm to hers and wrapping his fingers around Kate's.

The sob in her throat waited there as she studied his hands. Rough like her father's. Big. Different from what she recalled from their teenage years. More serious, somehow.

"I guess that's why I came here to talk to your mom. I wanted to see if she'd be open to letting me meet Clara."

"And she said no?" Kate's frown deepened.

"Not exactly. She wasn't cruel, either. Just honest. She reminded me that even you hadn't asked to renege on the deal. She asked what I would say. What I could offer Clara. She asked what the fallout might be, and she asked if I thought it could affect how Clara saw her world."

"And what did you say?" Kate pressed, amazed at this moment of history that she was entirely oblivious to. It made her feel inadequate and useless to know that while she was moving on with her life, poor Matt was back here dwelling on the past. Without her and without any support.

"I didn't have the answers. And when I didn't have the answers, she told me something that I didn't understand then."

"What?" Kate's voice betrayed a need for urgency.

Matt cleared his throat. "She said I had better get over it. And she said—and I'll never forget this, Kate—she said to me that she'd been in my shoes before and that she knew best."

"My mother had been in your shoes? What in the world does that mean?" Kate let go of his hand and a chill ran between them. The kitchen door stood open. No breeze swooped in from the screen. Just the warm summer air, hanging outside like a line of wash. She shivered against the fever of what her mother might have been hiding all those years.

Chapter 15—Clara

"I found something."

Clara tapped the speaker icon on her phone just as she pulled the door shut behind her and locked it. Part of her wanted to stay at the cottage for the night, but with the notebook now in her possession, her body was buzzing.

"What are you talking about?" Kate asked. She sounded different. *Distracted.*

Skipping down the path toward her car, Clara pulled the journal from her arm and again examined the exterior. "At the cottage," she replied. "I *found* something." For whatever reason, divulging what she thought she found felt too big to say.

"Oh!" Kate answered with sudden recognition, as though she'd been swinging on a birch tree, blissfully detached from Earth for a while. "Right. The *cottage*. What? What is it?"

"Um," Clara began, fumbling her way into her car and plopping into the seat with exhaustion. "Can we meet? For a drink, maybe?"

"Oh," Kate said again. Clara began to wonder if she'd woken her up from a deep sleep. She was acting so oddly.

After a beat, Clara raised her voice—only just. "*Hel-lo*? Kate? Are ya there?"

"Sorry, right. Yes. I'm here. Sorry, Clara. I just have someone here taking a look at the Inn."

Clara smiled and shook her head. Kate's budding project was destined to consume her. Maybe Clara ought to have called Amelia instead. She opened her mouth to say as much, but Kate went on.

"Do you normally *drink*?" Kate asked.

"No," Clara replied. "But I have a feeling we might need one."

***

They met at The Bottle, an eccentric wine bar at the far edge of Birch Village. Clara wasn't a big fan of The Bottle—too uppity—but Fiorillo's was out of the question and neither she nor Kate was willing to go to one of the dives inland or The Lake Shack, a tacky tourist trap closer to the marina.

The Bottle had been Nora's go-to spot.

The only way Clara could describe the interior decor was Nantucket Chic. Sailing and boating photographs (in disappointing shades of black and white) hung evenly along the walls. Dark wood furniture, in sparse measure, sat in orderly circles across a hardwood floor. A comically large helm held court at the wall nearest the lake and on either side of that, grand bay windows.

The bar, shining cleanly from a long stretch at the far side of the room, separated them from two white-shirted barkeeps (is that what you called them if it was a wine bar?). The hostess, a girl probably younger than Clara, stared with boredom, even as Clara and Kate stepped inside. Still, she mustered a snobbish smile. "Welcome to The Bottle. Is it just the two of you this evening?" she asked as Clara and Kate stepped up to her glass stand.

Kate, steely eyed, had no time for this woman's pretense. "Yes, and we'll take the seat by the window." She pointed to the right of the helm and began walking before the hostess had a chance to grab two thick drink menus. If there was one thing Kate and Clara had in common, it was a distaste for being treated like tourists. Amelia and Megan hated it, too. Come to think of it, no local appreciated the treatment.

Once they were seated and had ordered the lightest, sweetest wine on the menu, Clara pulled her bag from the back of the chair.

"So, what is it?" Kate asked as she propped her elbows on the polished tabletop.

Clara hesitated momentarily, clutching the journal in her hand before sliding it out of her leather bag and pressing it firmly onto the spot in front of her. She kept it there, anchored in place as she looked from it to Kate. Clara sighed. "I think it's Mom's—*Nora's*, I mean—I think it's her diary."

Kate's eyes grew wide, and she immediately reached across. "Are you serious? Let me see."

Swallowing, Clara pulled it in toward herself. "Hang on," she answered, feeling foolish and dramatic even though she was trying to be the exact opposite. "Maybe we need to wait until Amelia and Megan are here. We should open it together, right?"

"Then why did you bring me here?" Kate spat back, now crossing her arms defensively.

"I don't want to be the one to hold it. I don't know. It feels like... like bad luck or something." Clara bit her lower lip and loosened her grip on the notebook.

Kate cocked her head, her features softening. "Bad luck? Come on, Clara. Have you opened it yet? Do you even know for sure that's what it is?"

Clara shook her head.

The waiter returned with their drinks, and Kate immediately rose her glass in a toast. Clara frowned with suspicion.

"To Mom," the older of the two began. Clara lifted her glass with a degree of uneasiness. Kate continued, "Who left us with more than a house on the harbor, a cottage on a creek, and rental properties. All those turn to dust in the end. Just like you and me, Clara. Nora Hannigan left far more than that for her four *daughters*." Kate overemphasized the last word, and Clara felt her cheeks grow hot and her shoulders relax at her sister's unending drive to make her feel loved.

"To *Mom*," Clara agreed, pushing her glass toward Kate's.

They each took a long sip, then Clara offered the notebook across the table. "Here. You're the oldest. You take this and set up a meeting. We're going to need all hands on deck."

***

Managing to set aside the matter of the notebook and enjoying a glass of wine was easier than Clara predicted. Kate was consumed by working on the house on the harbor, or as she continued to refer it, the *Inn*. Clara giggled each time.

After her oldest sister (she'd never stop calling Kate her sister) finished walking her through what she'd accomplished, she admitted that she was indeed distracted when Clara had called her to get together.

"Matt," Kate confessed, pretending to hide behind her wine glass.

Clara didn't find it funny. "Matt Fiorillo?" There were no other Matts in their lives, of course, but the confirmation felt important. Kate nodded. "Was it about...?" Clara began, aiming an index finger at herself.

"No, no. Of course not," Kate replied, then turned sheepish. "Well, I mean—" she sighed and shook her head. "Clara, anything Matt and I have to talk about inevitably has to do with you, actually. And yes, to be frank we did talk about you." The tone shifted, and Clara could have sworn the lights grew dimmer in the already dark bar.

"Oh?" she studied her wine glass, focusing all her energy on a little line of bubbles at the top of the liquid and how it reminded her of a translucent caterpillar. She wanted to crawl into a hole, not discuss her origins.

Kate's fingers appeared in her vision. She was reaching out to hold Clara's hand, but Clara kept staring at the bubbles.

"Clara, it's okay. It was a good conversation. I called him initially to help with working on the Inn. But we had a good talk, too. A little about Mom. A little about *you*. It helped clear some things up for me."

At that, Clara lifted her eyes. "Like what?"

Kate smiled. "Did you know that Matt came to see if we were selling the house on the harbor?"

"Yes."

"He didn't want to buy it—well, I mean... he *did* if we were selling it. He was worried you weren't going to get as much as us. I guess years ago he came to the house to talk to Mom. He wanted to meet you. She wouldn't let him, and it turned him off of her. I suppose he sort of held a grudge about it. He worried about you, Clara."

"He could have come talked to me when I moved out," Clara reasoned, feeling like a mopey teenager with a Disney Dad who started a new family elsewhere. It was partially true. Matt had a daughter. A *different* daughter.

Kate nodded. "*If* you had moved out. But you never did. And he didn't know anything about you."

"True," Clara admitted. After all, Matt Fiorillo, though born and bred in Birch Harbor just like the Hannigan girls, had laid down his roots offshore on Heirloom Island, a miniature chunk of land just south of Heirloom Cove where the House on the Harbor sat. From what Clara knew now, he flipped houses all over the county but kept to himself. He sent his eighth-grade daughter, Viviana, to the private Catholic school on the island, further sequestering them from the mainstream.

Then again, Clara herself wasn't so mainstream. To school and home and that was that. She didn't go out. She didn't fraternize with other teachers. College was hard enough. There, she barely survived the raucous roommate she had in the dorm for two years before choosing to finish her degree online as much as possible. It wasn't out of fear that Clara shrunk from society. It was out of habit. Having been raised as a runtish only child to a woman who'd lost her husband years back and got trapped in a midlife crisis from age fifty on, Clara was odd at best. Her physical beauty kept her from being an outright weirdo, it seemed, but she got along best with books and a fresh set of crochet needles, unlike her social-media-obsessed peers.

"Anyway, whenever you're ready, maybe we can get together. You, me, and Matt?" Kate asked at last.

After nodding in uncomfortable agreement, Clara opted to change the conversation. "I met a guy today," she admitted. It came out all wrong, though. What she *wanted* to say was that she met her favorite student's father. But that's not how it sounded, and now she was outed.

Kate nearly choked on her wine. "What? What do you mean you *met a guy*? I have never in my life known you to be interested in men. I seriously thought you might go the *Nun* route after high school." A goofy smile spread across Kate's face as she rambled, and Clara desperately wanted to match it with her own, but she was too humiliated by her own misspeak.

Backpedaling, Clara waved her hands. "I mean... I met one of my students' parents. He works at the marina. He could help with the dock reno at the Inn." Clara shrugged and took a sip, looking out the window with as much nonchalance as she could put on.

"One question. Is he *hot*?"

"Ew!" Clara shrieked in response. "Don't ever use that word again!"

Kate rocked back in her seat and cackled gleefully. "I may be your biological mother, but I'm not your *mom*. Come on, Clara. I never even said I needed help with the dock. So, spill."

At that, Clara finally broke. Grinning broadly, she swirled her wine, swallowed the last of it then shook her head playfully. "He's the father of a teenager, for starters."

"Is he *single*?"

"Are you asking for yourself?" Clara shot Kate a coy look.

"I'm asking for *you*," Kate replied. "After all, I have my own prospect now."

Chapter 16—Megan

Megan decided to pack an overnight bag for the day trip to Birch Harbor. Just in case.

As she finished zipping it, her phone rang from the kitchen. Brian was at work, and Sarah was at school. Megan jogged from the living room to snatch up the receiver from the counter—she loved having a landline still... it felt safe.

"Hello?"

"I called you last night. I texted you. We are starting to panic up here." It was Kate.

Megan let out a sigh. She hadn't checked her phone since before bed the evening prior.

***

Their night had been busy. First a blow-out argument with Sarah over the trip (despite Megan's reminders that the teenager *wanted* to go to Birch Harbor). Then Brian acting weird and begging Megan to "talk" about things.

She gave in, but it resulted in nil. Instead, they agreed to watch JEOPARDY! together, which was weird. Megan had fallen asleep on the sofa only to be woken up by a gentle nudge. After startling in bewilderment at the touch (those last few months had been particularly cold), she thanked him and trudged up to her room, the master bedroom.

Not thinking twice about the fact that Brian was following her in there, she flopped into bed and let her eyes roll shut. Then, she felt a second nudge. This one different.

Desperate for sleep, she had murmured a *hm* or a *what* only to hear his voice again—*Brian's*. At that, her eyes shot open and panic flashed behind them. The last time he'd stepped foot in the master bedroom was to accuse her of taking his favorite tie about three weeks back. Otherwise, he kept to the guest room and out of her life.

"Is it *Sarah*?" Megan had whispered.

Brian squatted down beside her, his hands hanging on the mattress dangerously near her elbows. She wanted to sit up, but instead just stared at him there, eye-to-eye. Bed level. Megan had jutted out her chin as far as possible to ward off any doubling.

"No, no," he whispered back. "She's fine."

"Then what is it?" Megan frowned now.

Brian's Adam's apple bobbed. He looked a bit like a child at that moment, but Megan didn't dare give in to whatever would come next. "I started to change my sheets this morning but forgot to pull them from the dryer."

She clicked her tongue, suppressing a dumb giggle. "So what? Get a different set."

"I can't find them," he replied, this time giving her a doghouse face—silly and pleading.

Megan sat up, now suddenly wide awake. "Are you... are you asking to sleep in here?"

Brian leaned back, his hands still gripping the mattress. Megan could not help but to take in her soon-to-be-ex-husband's white t-shirt. It pulled taut against his body. It wasn't the body he had when he was twenty. But it was the body of the father of her daughter. The man who provided for them. The one who wanted to visit her mother's gravesite.

"Megan, I can't sleep on that bed anymore," he replied. Megan thought she saw a flicker in his eyes. Sincerity in some form. Brian pressed a hand to his back and winced. "It kills my back. You know that."

"What about the sofa?"

He balked.

Oh well, Megan thought to herself. It was a king-sized bed. She *could* have suggested that he just sign the paperwork, they sell the house, and he buys his own new house with a new bed.

But she didn't.

Instead, the woman who'd been bracing for a divorce threw back the covers and said, "Get in here."

***

"Sorry," Megan replied breathlessly, glancing around the kitchen for her coffee mug. "Busy night. What's up?" Color flooded her cheeks, and she was thankful Kate couldn't see her.

"Clara found something that we all need to take a look at."

Having found her mug next to her computer, in the den, Megan took it back to the kitchen and wedged the phone between her ear and shoulder. "What is it?"

"We think it's Mom's diary or journal."

"What do you mean you *think*?"

Kate's voice dropped an octave. "I know it is, but Clara is being weird about peeking inside without you and Amelia present."

Megan rolled her eyes. "Why is Clara being weird?" It seemed the more concerning detail of the news.

"Once bitten, twice shy?"

It made sense. In fact, Megan was surprised Clara was holding up as well as she was. Perhaps that had to do with a fulfilling career and a beautiful home to move into. As Megan had learned quickly, security equated to happiness. Now if only she could secure a little of that...

"Okay, so did you read it?" Megan asked.

"No, I just flipped to the front page to see it matched the four pages we got from the estate. I told Clara I'd wait until we all got together."

"And when will that be?"

"Aren't you coming to town tomorrow?"

Megan sighed. "Yes, but we sort of have plans." Her mind flicked to Brian and Sarah and the ensuing road trip. It would be painful and awkward, and she began to regret forcing Sarah to skip her last day of school for the occasion. Maybe it was unfair. Blinking, she added, "Maybe we can change things up. Are you all willing to wait one day?"

"Yes, of course. I have a ton to do," Kate answered. Megan detected relief in her voice, and it occurred to her that of the four of them not a single one was anxious to dive back into the annals of Nora Hannigan.

"Okay, how about this. I'll talk to Brian tonight. His conference doesn't start until Friday. I can drive down in the morning, and he can bring Sarah after school tomorrow. She and I will still be at the house—Er... the *Inn*—and Brian can take off after he pays his respects."

"Will he agree to that?"

"If he doesn't, then I'll have to figure something else out."

"Just come without him," Kate suggested.

Megan bit her lower lip. "It'll be fine. I think he'll agree."

Kate's voice lightened. "Okay, it's settled. We'll get together tomorrow morning and hash out the journal. Breakfast here?"

"Make it brunch." And with that, Megan clicked off and dashed upstairs to get her cell phone. She needed to text her husband.

Their plans had changed.

Chapter 17—Amelia

After agreeing with Kate that they'd put together a sister brunch to examine the journal—all of which Amelia felt was incredibly melodramatic—she could turn her attention to Michael and their research project. But only after fulfilling her promise to Kate to help around the house that morning.

Amelia scraped the remnants of her egg whites into the garbage disposal. "Okay, what's the plan?" she asked, wiping her hands on the coarse dish towel that hung from the cabinet door beneath the sink.

Kate joined her there, dumping half a cup of coffee into the sink and rinsing both the mug and Amelia's plate with a quick spray of water. "Okay, so I have the basics set up to open as an Air B&B. I worked on that last night. To open as a full-service bed-and-breakfast—I mean the real deal—well, that'll take a while. I figure in the interim, why not make some money and get our names out there?" Kate flashed a white smile at Amelia, who felt happy for her sister.

Smiling back, Amelia prodded her on. "That's a great idea. What's the plan?"

"Come take a look." Kate waved Amelia to the parlor where the evening before they had hauled up an antique dresser with the help of Michael and Matt. Early that morning, Amelia heard Kate rummaging around downstairs, and it was evident that this was her project: a reception desk, just off the front hall on the threshold between the foyer and the parlor. It was a snug fit, but it looked just right.

A green Tiffany lamp the likes of which Amelia had never appreciated as a teenager, shone dimly on Kate's small laptop. The old wood of the dresser shined under a fresh layer of polish.

Amelia wondered how she missed the little set up when she dragged herself down for breakfast that morning.

"Kate, this is amazing," she gushed, rounding the hulking dresser-desk and finding a wobbly, three-legged stool behind it. "Hey, that's

Grandma Hannigan's old chair." She ran her hand over the thick hand-upholstered seat. It was stained and rickety, but she recognized it immediately from when her grandmother had once scolded her for sitting on it.

Amelia-Ann! That's not a sitting chair! the old woman had cried out.

At the time, Amelia had wondered what it was for if not for sitting. Later, her mother would explain that Grandma Hannigan liked things a certain way, and some of the furniture were antiques and just for looking at, not enjoying. It was at that moment that Amelia knew she'd never be the sort to buy furniture *just for looking*. She'd buy it for sitting on it and enjoying it, like any other *normal* person. The admonishment and her mother's defense thereof was one of those moments in a child's life that shapes who she becomes. Amelia believed that firmly.

"This is not a sitting chair," she murmured, falling back to that moment from so long ago.

"What?" Kate asked.

"Oh," Amelia laughed lightly. "I just remember Grandma Hannigan yelling at me for sitting on this when I was a kid. She said it wasn't a sitting chair."

Kate appeared to take Amelia's memory seriously. "I knew it was hers, but she never told me that," she commented.

"Probably because you were so well-behaved. You naturally knew right from wrong, even when it was illogical like a no-sitting chair. No one was ever worried *you* would ruin anything."

Silence fell between them. What Amelia said was filled with great, retrospective irony, and they both knew it. Amelia flicked a glance to her sister, waiting for her to snap back defensively.

Kate did not snap back, however. Instead, she laughed, a deep belly laugh. Amelia made a face, waiting for the laughter to turn to tears, but it didn't.

"Ah, so you are proud to be a rebel?" Amelia joked, crossing her arms.

"I was never a rebel. I was... I was..."

"You were in love," Amelia whispered, smiling sadly for her sister.

Kate stopped laughing entirely, and her face fell. Although, she didn't seem upset.

Shaking it off seemed easy enough, and Kate joined Amelia in the cramped space behind the dresser. "Here, look," she said to Amelia, waking up her laptop and navigating to a landing page.

Amelia squinted at the screen. Kate had drawn up a listing on the Air B&B website. It was her own. Amelia flashed a grin at her older sister then read on.

Welcome to the Heirloom Inn of Birch Harbor! Quaint individual guest rooms are now available in this historic, lakeside home on Heirloom Cove. Perfect for a cozy waterfront weekend and complete with easy-access full bathrooms. Enjoy the stunning sunrise on our well-appointed deck or take Grandpa Hannigan's old kayak out for a whirl to nearby Heirloom Island. Prefer to relax? Find your favorite snoozing place in an Adirondack chair on our private beach. Full breakfast offered daily in addition to brunch-time and afternoon snacks and evening wine and cheese, sourced locally. Finally, the Heirloom Inn is a short walk to Birch Village Marina, where guests can dine, drink, shop, and boat any day of the week. Don't miss out on your best weekend getaway yet. Book with Kate Hannigan today.

"Oh, Kate," Amelia breathed the words as she clicked through a couple images Kate had uploaded. "And these photos. Kate, you were *meant* for this," Amelia beamed, finally tearing her eyes from the screen.

"You like it?" Kate asked, her eyebrows scrunching lines into her forehead.

"Like it? It's perfect."

"Do I oversell it?"

Amelia considered that. For the time being, Kate didn't have a fully functional bed-and-breakfast in the modern sense. Her guest rooms were their childhood bedrooms. And locally sourced wine and cheese? She tapped her chin with her finger. "I believe in you, Kate," she said at last, recalling every other time someone in her life had reminded her that dreams were dreams. If someone had told Amelia they believed in her, too, maybe she'd be more than a bit-part actress in off-the-beaten-path theatres. "But," she began to add, an idea forming in her mind. "I think you could use one more thing for this reception stand."

"What?" Kate asked, frowning through her growing excitement.

"A brochure stand."

"Huh?"

"If I were coming to town, I would want to know where I could catch a show or what restaurant you recommend."

"I can just tell them that. No need for a brochure. That's too... *motel*."

A giggle fell out of Amelia's mouth. "Okay, fair. But you should probably have a list or something to *reference*."

Kate cocked her head. "I wouldn't have thought of that. It's sort of a minor thing, though. Right?"

"Take it from someone who rushes into grand ideas with little success. You want to think of everything in advance." Amelia couldn't believe she had to remind her older sister of this. Kate was the organized one. The detail person. The perfectionist.

"True. Let's chat over gardening. I need to till the front beds and head up to the nursery this morning. Maybe you can give me a rundown of local attractions."

"Ha," Amelia scoffed. "Birch Harbor has the *lake*. That's it."

"What about that community theatre Michael and Clara mentioned? Have you looked into that?" Kate literally elbowed Amelia, who realized exactly where the line of conversation was going.

"I haven't pursued that angle," she said, sighing.

"Well what angle *have* you pursued?" Kate gave her a knowing look.

Amelia's voice sharpened to a point. "I'm pursuing the matter of our missing father, actually."

Chapter 18—Kate

The nursery didn't open until nine, but Kate and Amelia arrived a few minutes early. Simply called Birches, it offered a good-sized garden and shop, and it was where Nora had come for everything she ever needed. Situated just on the inland side of Birch Avenue from the Village, the women could have walked there if they'd rolled a wagon with them, but Kate couldn't find the rusty Red Flyer she had recalled from her childhood.

So instead, she threw a paint sheet down in the back of the SUV and drove it the short way. Amelia had hopped out and stretched like she'd been cooped up then twirled around in the sunlight. Kate smiled at her younger sister. A dreamer in every sense of the word.

It was probably Kate's job to help the girl find a path, but if Amelia wouldn't take her advice, then it was a futile attempt.

They leaned together against the hood, waiting for the owners to open the front gates.

"Have you heard from Jimmy?" Kate asked while she chewed on a painful hangnail.

The sun warmed Kate's back. It would be nice to spend the afternoon under an umbrella on the beach. Maybe she would if she finished her garden plans and drew up a list of local attractions like Amelia had suggested. It was a good idea that Kate *had* considered. She wanted her sister to feel like she was helpful. Necessary, even, so she feigned ignorance. In fact, Kate would have a little checklist and information stowed neatly in a Word document for when her guests inquired. Maybe she'd even upload it to a website, if she ever developed one. But she did believe that handing out a half sheet upon check-in didn't fit the quaint, homey experience she hoped to offer.

Her mind began to wander off to Matt, who was coming by after he handled some morning business. He didn't install new air conditioning units, but he agreed to see if he could fix the current one. If not, they'd go together to order a unit and schedule the installation at Harbor Hardware.

Beside Kate, Amelia kicked at an errant green leaf then answered. "Heck *no*, I have not spoken to Jimmy. He was an easy one to boot."

Smiling, Kate patted Amelia's shoulder. "I'm proud of you." Amelia was the type to date a guy for a year or so, break up (or rather, be dumped), meet someone similar to the last, enter a new relationship right off the bat, dive deep, break up, and so on into a long, deep cycle that revealed how unwilling she was to be alone. Of course, the pretty brunette had terrible taste. For nearing middle age, she looked closer to thirty-five and therefore attracted men south of thirty, even.

Once the guy found out Amelia's real age, it went one of two ways. He was normal enough to quit then. Or, he was immature enough to pursue the cougar-style fling. What Kate never could figure out was why Amelia didn't go for men her own age.

Then again, perhaps that was the wrong question.

"What about Michael?" The words fell out of Kate's mouth. An accident. She hadn't planned to bring it up, because all of them had been there, done that. Suggested Amelia try this nice man or that and with zero success. Amelia was the sort who needed to stumble along herself, pushing away help like a four-year-old.

To Kate's surprise, Amelia didn't make a face or slap away the question. Instead, she smiled. "He's handsome, that's true."

The two shared a look, a dash of bewilderment, a hint of glee. Kate nodded. "He *is* handsome."

"But he's not my type." There it was. The batting away of a great idea.

Kate just sighed.

"Actually, that's not it." Amelia pushed off the SUV and walked a short distance away and back, flapping her hands gently along her jeans.

"What do you mean?" Kate watched her sister, who looked more nervous than petulant.

"I think I'm not *his* type. That's what I mean."

Kate frowned. A truth materialized in Amelia's words, something dark and deep. Kate was about to answer with a word or two of encouragement, but somebody shuffled behind the gate, jiggling the chain and cutting short what could have been an important conversation.

***

Back at the Inn, the sisters worked efficiently to unload the SUV. Tansy and thistle, shrubs, and a couple young trees sat patiently in their plastic pots, awaiting the delicate process of transplantation into their forever home.

"Start now or snack first?" Amelia asked, propping her hands on her hips.

Kate clicked her tongue. "All we've done so far is shop. We're starting."

Together, they began clearing the planters and churning soil in silence. Kate didn't mind pulling deep-rooted weeds. She was good at it. Amelia seemed to struggle, so Kate directed her to start measuring and spacing out holes for the new selection.

"So," Amelia broke the quiet, her voice light. "Are you going to get a sign or something like that?" She heaved back on her heels and stared up at the house. Kate mimicked her then twisted around to study the road.

"I'm not sure. I want to keep it homey; you know?"

"You could do something tasteful and simple. Just something that says The Heirloom House."

"It's the Heirloom *Inn*," Kate corrected, feigning exasperation. She knew she was being a little militant about a business name that wasn't even *real* yet, so she tried for levity, but her tone came out edgy instead, and Amelia just rolled her eyes. "Anyway," Kate went on, "that's a good idea. Maybe something small. Like a little wooden placard hanging from a post. Like an old-fashioned business that happens to be nestled in a family neighborhood."

"Well, this is the property nearest the marina, so it wouldn't be odd to have a sign. People might even think this place is a business rather than a house, especially because it's so big."

"But those are all homes." Kate pointed down the shoreline at the other houses, spaced generously apart, that unfurled all the way past the town limits. She turned and went back to weeding, tugging hard at a stubborn and gnarly root.

Amelia resumed digging. "Can we put on some music?" she asked. "I'm getting a little bored."

Kate laughed. "You are so... *you*," she observed. "Is there ever quiet in your head?"

"I hate to have quiet in my head," Amelia admitted, grinning mischievously. "I mean we could gossip if you want instead, but I have a hard time being alone with my thoughts."

Kate's smile washed away, and she rubbed a line of sweat from her brow. "Well, let me ask you this."

Amelia arched an eyebrow.

The root in Kate's hand loosened, and she sailed backward, falling on her butt as she lifted the stickery green weed in victory above her head. They both chuckled, but Kate tossed it to the pile with the others, patted her hands off on the knees of her yoga pants and grabbed the nearest thistle, returning to Amelia to begin the transplant. "Amelia," she started, treading carefully. "You said you didn't think you were Michael's type. How do you know?"

"Why? Are you interested in him, too?"

"Oh, so you *are* interested," Kate jabbed a finger into Amelia's shoulder playfully, and the latter shook her head and then threw it back, laughing at herself. "All right, all right. You caught me. I think he's hot, what can I say! And he's smart and interesting. A little elusive, maybe. Dark and brooding. Older."

"Older?" Kate shot back. "He's *our* age, for crying out loud!"

Amelia laughed again, and Kate beamed back. They were on track again. It was just the sort of conversation they needed to break the ice and get down to it.

Shaking her head and helping pull apart the roots of the thistle, Amelia answered. "I can't imagine he would go for a flighty actress-type. You know?"

"Opposites attract." Kate pulled a bag of topsoil over, tearing a hole into the top with her car key then ripping the plastic wide enough to dump some dirt into the hole. They set about patting the fresh earth in around the plant.

"You have to have something in common, even a little something. We don't."

"Who knows? Maybe you do. He's interested in this little family mystery, after all. Right?"

"Well everyone loves a good mystery. And anyway, the only reason I'm invested is because it's Wendell. Our own father. What stake could Michael really have."

Kate stopped patting and smiled at her little sister. "Maybe he's bored, too."

***

"Hey there." The voice came from behind the women as they sat like schoolgirls, giggling themselves into fits of laughter. Tears streamed down Kate's face and her sides ached in blissful hysteria, but she managed to turn and wipe the wetness away. Her gaze focused on Matt.

"Hi," she finally said, standing and brushing dirt and dying weeds from her behind. "Come on in." She waved him through the gate of the white picket fence.

He smiled and lifted his hands. "Can I get in on this joke?"

Amelia's laughter finally died off. "I'll go brew some tea and slice up that watermelon. It's definitely *snack* time now." Kate began to thank her, but Amelia then had the gall to *wink* at her. A fat, goofy wink that Matt also had the burden of witnessing.

Kate flushed a deep red and apologized profusely, but he didn't let it go and instead played dim.

"What was that for?" he asked, grinning and dipping his chin in Kate's direction. She could have melted then and there. She could have died of humiliation. But life was too short, and she'd been a party to too much heartache of late.

So, she played right along.

"Oh, the wink?" she answered boldly. "She thinks I like you again."

Clearly unprepared to be pushed to the defensive, Matt fell back a step, laughing awkwardly. "This feels a little like déjà vu. Wasn't it Amelia who set us up in the first place?"

"Inadvertently," Kate allowed. "She's the one who blew my cover at that party." Kate cringed inside. She'd never been a cool kid at school. And *never* a partier. But so many decades ago, when she was just a sophomore and Amelia was only in middle school, one of Amelia's so-called friends caught word that the Hannigan parents were out of town for the weekend. Matt, being more connected to various social circles at Birch Harbor High, showed up and slipped into the corner of the back deck. It was the same place Amelia and Megan were hiding, two little girls, watching on as high schoolers whooped and laughed, played music and danced. Nothing too nefarious happened that night, but only because Kate frantically policed the whole event, monitoring guests and turning the music down every ten minutes.

At one point during that night, Amelia and Megan had grown confident. They began strutting around the place like Kate should have, flirting with the older boys and munching on potato chips between casual sips of soda.

Near the end of the function, while Kate was plucking plastic cups and wadded napkins from the back of the sofa, Matt had wandered inside. Matt Fiorillo, the boy she'd swooned over since forever. The one whose name was doodled in pretty swirls across otherwise empty pages on her desk in her bedroom. The one she confided about to her sisters, bragging that his parents owned the Italian restaurant at the Village.

Kate could picture the moment, and she was certain Matt could too. They were frozen alone in the living room, her with a white plastic bag, him with his hands shoved deep in his pockets. He said hi. She said hi. He thanked her for a great party. She pretended that it was her original goal and accepted his gratitude, coolly, unwilling to admit that it was another girl who made everything come together. Another organized girl. A more social one. Not Kate.

Then a little voice piped in from the doorway behind them. It had been Amelia, of course, the one more willing to intrude. She'd told Matt that Kate was in love with him.

In every other scenario in which such a mortifying event would have taken place across the late-night living rooms of America, it would have been game over right then and there.

But it wasn't.

Matt had sort of glowed as Kate shouted at her sister to bug off. And then, like a fairy tale, he kissed her. Right there in the living room, while teenagers meandered across the back deck and down toward the beach. Her with a plastic trash bag. Him with a secret crush.

It was probably the best night of Kate's life. Other than her wedding day and the birth of her children. It was the sort of night that only happened in movies or great books. The perfect moment. Too perfect, she remembered thinking later. Fate-filled and star-crossed. A modern-day *Romeo and Juliet*. Minus the double suicide, sure. Different tragedies eventualized. A deeply guarded secret. The adoption of their untimely child. And heartbreak that only young love could know.

Kate felt the heat of the sun on her neck. She was no teenager in the dim light of the living room lamp, her face clear and body thin and supple. Now she was a widow. A mother of two. Or three—depending on which stat you went by. An orphan, too, by all accounts.

Yet, for all that had changed, Kate's heart was the same it always had been. It longed for him just the same. It throbbed now, just the same as it did that night. Their first kiss.

She rubbed the back of her arm against her forehead, smearing dirt and sweat, no doubt. But Kate felt pretty. Not for how she looked but for how she was being looked upon.

By the man who always was the love of her life. There, at the place she now called home.

"Kate," Matt murmured. "Am I here to help you with the house or am I here for another reason?" His tone began playfully enough but slipped into a lower octave, betraying the same sincere question she'd been asking herself ever since she called him for help.

"Well," she began, twisting around to admire the place. She had a lot of work ahead of her, and only some of it would belong to him or another repairman. "That depends."

"On what?"

"On your availability, for starters," she replied.

He crossed his arms over his chest and shifted his weight onto one leg, grinning. "All right," Matt answered. "I have three projects in the works. One inland, one on the island, and I'm working on St. Rita's in town, building all new pews."

"That sounds like a no," Kate answered, confused. Earlier, he seemed excited to help. Insistent, too.

"But those are all business. Well, except for St. Rita's. That's a passion project, so to speak."

"This would be business, too," Kate argued.

He shook his head. "This is family. And I'm always available for *family*."

Chapter 19—Clara

"I would have liked to sleep in," Clara mumbled as she joined Kate and Amelia in the kitchen of the house on the harbor—or rather... the *Inn*. "It's my first day of summer."

"Sleep in? It's after nine," Kate replied, pushing a fresh mug of coffee across the island.

"You have no idea the exhaustion of a teacher after the last day of school. And with fourteen-year-olds at the *lake*. It's more stressful than conducting brain surgery, I'm fairly positive."

Through a bite of bacon, Amelia nodded her head sympathetically. "I could see that. You have to play lifeguard *and* parent to what... twenty kids?"

"Try a hundred! The whole eighth grade goes. There were fewer than eight adults. It's totally insane. I can't believe parents sign off on it."

"I'm sure the kids had a blast," Kate said twirling away from the stove with a heaping plate of fluffy scrambled eggs. Clara's mouth watered immediately.

She smiled to herself. The kids *did* have a blast. Even meek little Mercy Hennings ventured out with a thick layer of sunscreen and a wide brim hat. She was such an enigma. Classically beautiful, smart, confident—she apparently took after her father in those respects—but painfully asocial. Then again, perhaps it wasn't that Mercy was asocial. Maybe she was just disinterested in her peers. She didn't quite see value in friendships, oddly. Mercy's studies were tantamount and therefore her most important relationships were with her teachers and one select other student, a shy, studious seventh grader who took eighth grade advanced math.

However, Mercy had let loose the day before—in so much as Mercy *would* let loose. She joined in a game of beach volleyball, surprising everyone with her athletic prowess, and even splashed in the water with a small group—the brainy eighth graders who were a little in awe of Mercy not only for her smarts but also for her beauty, no doubt. By and large, the child was sort of... untouchable. But not to Clara.

Clara often wondered if she was a bit like Mercy as a child. It was hard to know. Even just a decade and a half set them in distant worlds. Mercy's was one entrenched in social media and 24-7 academic, social, familial, and personal pressure. Clara's was one in which the academic and social pressure existed only inside the four walls of the school building. At home, she was a little Cinderella figure, helping her past-her-prime single mother with cleaning and turning over the apartments. Nora never took much of a genuine interest in Clara's academics, but that had also been true of Kate, Amelia, and Megan. Nora preferred ice cream socials to parent-teacher conferences and Parents Night Out over the Regional Spelling Bee. Even so, Nora was not abusive or even aloof. She loved and cared for all her children. They were close.

"The kids had a ball. It was worth falling into bed at six last night." She laughed lightly. "And anyway, I wouldn't miss *this* for the world. When does Megan get in?"

Amelia glanced toward the door. "She should be here any time. She had to change plans, but it sounds like, from what Kate said, she's coming to town alone, then Brian and Sarah are driving in to meet her. Then Brian is leaving Sarah here," Amelia pointed her finger down, "to help with the reno—"

"Wait a minute, back up." Clara held up her palm. "Brian is coming to Birch Harbor? Why?"

The older two exchanged an unreadable expression.

"What?" Clara asked. "What is it?"

Kate slipped a serving spoon beneath the pile of eggs and doled out plates. "Well, Amelia and I are wondering the same thing as you."

Amelia served herself a couple scoops of eggs then added a slice of bacon. "According to Megan, Brian regretted not coming to Mom's funeral. I guess it's eating him alive or whatever. So, he told her he was going to visit her burial site."

Clara's jaw hit the ground, but Amelia kept going.

"Well, Megan thought that would be 'weird,'" she inserted air quotes, which Clara inwardly rolled her eyes at, "so she said she was coming with him. So, they are meeting there later today."

"Oh no," Kate covered her mouth with one hand.

"What? What is it?" Amelia dropped her fork. A look of panic shadowed her features.

"It's just that... we were going to have lunch together. With Matt and Brian."

"Matt *and* Brian?"

Confusion swirled in the kitchen as they twittered back and forth for a moment until a voice broke their attention.

"Yes. Dinner would be better."

Kate, Amelia, and Clara jerked their heads to the front hall. "Megan," Amelia uttered.

Clara watched in fascination as Megan, clad in sleek black yoga pants, a fitted black tank, and purple tennis shoes strode in. The raven-haired forty-something tightened her ponytail and tossed an overnight bag onto the floor by the pantry. "I'm starving," she declared, eyeing the kitchen island without so much as a greeting.

"Let's eat, then we can get started on the matter at hand." Clara led by example, moving her mug to the table then filling her plate with eggs, fresh fruit, and a couple of thin, greasy slices of bacon.

Once they were all sitting, Megan cleared her throat. "So, what exactly *is* the matter at hand?"

"What do you mean?" Clara narrowed her eyes on the notebook which sat conspicuously in front of Kate's place setting.

Megan took a long swig of coffee, seemed to swish it in her mouth, which made Clara want to gag, then explained herself. "We've got the lighthouse issue, which by the way doesn't add up. If that place were left to us, your lawyer boyfriend would know about it," she indicated Amelia by tapping her finger through the air. Clara looked at Amelia whose eyes grew wide. She was about to protest, but Megan went on. "And this project." She twirled her finger around the kitchen. "Our hometown B and B."

Clara smiled at Kate knowingly. She was proud of her oldest sister for following her dream, and they were all excited to see what became of it. At that moment, it dawned on Clara that Megan's story was hanging in the air like an open quotation mark. Just a beginning. No ending or even hope of one—at least regarding where life was about to take her. Or, rather, where she was going to take life.

"And now Mom's secret diary? I feel like I'm living in a Lifetime movie." Megan shrugged and took another long swig. Clara and the other two laughed at her joke, but it was the truth.

"And," Clara added, sharpening the word with her tone. "Your so-called divorce to the man you've just invited for an overnight getaway."

"*And*," Amelia joined in, playing along, "we never did learn if you got that confidential gig with Mistletoe."

"Mistletoe?" Clara asked, confusion twisting her features.

Megan's steely facade melted, and she shot Amelia a look. "You want me to go first? Fine, I'll go first." To an outsider, Megan would seem edgy and out of sorts. But her sisters knew that this version of Megan was an inspired one. She was on the brink of something. Something exciting, probably. It was the exact same way Brian would get—worked up, amped. Clara noticed this about him from a young age. At Christmas, before Sarah opened her gifts, Brian would shush everyone, and his knee would begin bouncing erratically from his seat on the edge of the sofa. Megan was just that way, too.

Clara, Kate, and Amelia sipped on their coffee and picked at their breakfast as they waited for Megan to swallow a big bite of eggs. "All right," she began through a mouthful, her cadence slowing down. "All right. So, for those of you here who don't know, I went out on a limb and applied for a job with this dating app. It's called Mistletoe. Cheesy, I know. *I know*. But, like, it's been my *dream* to do matchmaking. If I could pick a career, I'd be that sassy reality TV woman. You know, the one who fixes up millionaires? I don't care about the glamour part; I just like slicing people down to their basic values. What makes us tick, all that. Right?" She paused to take a sip, and Clara eyed Kate and Amelia, both who bore amused expressions.

"So," Megan continued, "this company, Mistletoe, had an opening for a social media associate, and since I have Sarah, who's a total pro, I thought it could work. Well, I didn't get the job." She pushed out a long breath, but her face didn't fall. Instead, she kept going. "And then Brian and I started sleeping together again."

"What!" Kate cried.

Clara gagged on her eggs. "Ew!"

"Yee-haw!" Amelia cheered.

Megan's face glowed. "No, no, no. Don't get too excited, geez. I mean he slept in our bed last night, instead of the guest room."

"So..." Amelia cut in, "is that a baby step toward reconciliation or...?"

Clara leaned forward, alarmed and charmed by the sudden switch in Megan's dark, dreary life.

"A *very* baby step. And no one said anything about reconciliation. The divorce is still on," Megan added, her face drawing into that of a schoolmarm. But the seed was planted. Maybe, despite the misfortune of not getting the job she'd told them about, Megan would come out ahead. That's what Clara liked to think. She was an optimist.

The sun that had been streaming in from the top of the kitchen window rose enough that Clara could lower her hand as she looked across to Megan. "So, what about a job?"

"I told you. I didn't get it."

Washed in naivete, Clara pressed the matter, genuinely curious about what Megan's plans *were*. "What do you think you'll do now?"

Kate and Amelia appeared interested in the answer. They each set their mugs down and kept mum for a moment, allowing Megan to wash down the last of her eggs with a long gulp of orange juice. She was such a *visceral* person, Megan. From her looks to her body language and mannerisms, she was the sort of woman who lived to the full limits of her existence. In fact, that was the characteristic that Amelia and Megan shared. It's what offset them from Kate. And, from Clara. It was a Nora feature, and one that Clara both admired and feared.

"I'm going to start my own darn matchmaking app, that's what I'll do," Megan replied, laughing after. "I'm kidding. I'll just keep my eyes open. Honestly, things just feel different for me. I can't put a finger on it... maybe it's the fact that we have a couple projects here, and it's summer now so I'm more available..." her voice trailed off.

"It's not a bad idea," Kate said, rising to clear her plate and silverware and patting Megan's shoulder en route to the sink.

"I don't have the slightest idea how to write software code or run a business. It's out of the question. We're moving on." And with that, Megan effectively ended the line of conversation Clara felt most invested in. Truth be told, the youngest of the four was dreading cracking into the journal. The last time they drove down this road, it resulted in the most painful revelation in which she'd ever been involved. She couldn't imagine that the woman who raised her had many other skeletons, but if she did, Clara was happy to live without knowing about them.

As if reading Clara's mind, Kate returned to the table, tucked herself onto a chair and pulled the diary to the spot where her breakfast plate had sat just moments before. "Okay," she started. "Who's ready for this?"

"Hold on," Amelia held up a hand. In her other one was her phone. "It's Michael."

"So?" Megan replied, settling into her seat and sipping from her black drink.

"He has information," Amelia answered, dropping the phone and meeting each of their gazes. The news felt ominous, though Clara didn't know why.

"What? About the lighthouse? Or about Wendell?" Clara asked, the name dancing on her tongue like an unfamiliar taste. She'd never known Wendell. All her life, up until just recently, she knew the man as her father, but that meant little when she hadn't so much as met him. To call him Dad now felt wrong. To call him Wendell felt odd. It was a lose-lose.

"Both?" Amelia answered in the form of a question.

Kate pressed her hand against the table nearer to Amelia's plate. "Well? What is he saying?"

"He said he found out the name of the person who pays property taxes for the lighthouse—both the light and the house." She glanced up again, a stumped expression filling her fair features.

"And is it Nora Hannigan?" Kate asked.

Amelia shook her head slowly, frowning deeply at her phone screen.

"Is it Kate?" Clara asked, her innocence and naivete emerging for a second time. That's how she always felt around her older sisters—like the baby of the family. Which, well, she was.

Again, Amelia shook her head.

"Is it *any* of us?" Megan set her coffee down with a thud and propped an elbow on the table, wagging a hand for Amelia to answer them.

Clara could see Amelia's neck roll up and down in a deep swallow before she answered. "It's someone else. Someone who lives in *Indiana*, he says."

Kate pushed air through her teeth. "What's their name?"

"Liesel Hart."

Chapter 20—Megan

The name didn't ring a bell for any of them, but Megan liked it. It reminded her of her favorite character from *The Sound of Music*. She set down her mug and spoke up. "So this person is a stranger? The Actons sold the property?"

Amelia held up a finger. "Let me call Michael. It's too hard to get important info from a text. Be right back." She glided out of the room, her phone pressed to her ear.

It gave the others a moment to confer.

"Why did Mom write that it belonged to us?" Clara's voice bordered on sounding whiny.

Megan needed a second cup of coffee if she was going to deal with this. "If we open the *journal*," she stabbed toward Kate's table front, "then maybe we'll *find out*." Her tone was sing-song sarcastic, as Kate used to put it. The two now exchanged a look. Laughter tugged at the edges of the conversation. It would appear each one was reverting to her childhood self. That's what happened when the Hannigan sisters came together. They fell back in time.

A smile broke out on Kate's mouth, but she shook her head. "Once Amelia's back, we will. Maybe Michael has more to tell her, though."

Refilling her coffee and this time adding a second dash of sugar, Megan slid her own phone from her bag on the floor and carried it to the table. Discreetly, she clicked it awake, finding two unread messages. One from Sarah. One from Brian.

To see both their names in her inbox felt a little like old times. When they first gave Sarah a cell phone, just a couple years back, it was normal and welcome for Megan to bounce messages back between the two individually. They also had a group chat they frequented. Then, that changed. The messages between Sarah and Megan grew more tense and less regular. Megan had blamed it all on teenagehood. But deep down, she knew there was more to it than that.

And the messages with Brian went through a similar phase until they nearly halted. More recently, if his name popped into her inbox, it gave Megan a stomachache or a headache or both at once.

Now, however, she felt fine. Happy, even, despite all the drama swirling around the old house in which she sat with her sisters, sipping on Kate's light roast coffee. She saved Brian's text and clicked on Sarah's first.

Can I stay at Clara's tonight?

Megan flicked a glance up at the petite blonde who sat next to her. Clara, too, was deep into a text conversation, it appeared.

"Are you talking to Sarah?" Megan asked.

Clara looked up. "Oh," color rushed to her cheeks. "Um, no." She fumbled her phone onto the table until it landed upside down with a thud. "Sorry. I was on Facebook."

Megan and Kate looked at each other, then back at their little sister. "Facebook?" Kate arched an eyebrow.

"It's nothing. I'll tell you later. What about Sarah?" Clara batted the air and her face returned to its normal tone.

Waving her own phone screen at Clara, Megan replied, "Sarah is asking if she can stay at your apartment with you?"

Clara's eyes lit up. "I'd *love* that! Maybe she can help me start moving stuff over and getting set up in the cottage?"

"Perfect," Megan replied, tapping out a quick reply to her daughter. She was about to open Brian's message when Amelia came back in the room, a triumphant look on her face.

Kate asked, "Well?"

Amelia grinned, hands on her hips. "Okay," she began, relaxing from her power pose and returning to the table and assuming a conspiratorial tone. "He said he's going to look deeper, but from what he can see this Liesel Hart *character* began paying property taxes upon the deaths of Grandma and Grandpa Acton. Dad never paid taxes, and he wasn't technically listed in their estate, we can assume. But that's not all."

The other three leaned in closer.

"Michael said that he found no record of sale."

"What does that mean?" Megan asked.

"He could see that the deed was transferred from a joint agreement between the Coast Guard and the county to a private entity in the early nineties. But that was before Grandma and Grandpa died."

Clara shifted in her seat. "And after they died, it wasn't sold?"

"Right. Michael said the property became private with that earlier transfer, but from what he can tell, the Actons never sold it."

Megan drew a finger to her mouth and began to chew on a hangnail. "So why is this Liesel person paying taxes on it?"

"We don't know. We'd have to get in touch with their estate attorney."

Kate piped up. "Does anyone remember who that was? I feel like I should know this. I mean, we were beneficiaries. Remember? We each got a little money when they passed."

"Right, but didn't their other relatives sort of take over?" Megan protested, her memory growing shades clearer as the conversation jogged it.

"Yes," Kate answered. "Their siblings saw to the arrangements. I think it was a brother who acted as the executor. Uncle Hugh, right?"

Megan didn't know any of that. She wasn't as in the loop as either Kate or Amelia, but surely this would be an easy mystery to solve. "Do you have his contact information?"

Kate's eyes flashed. "Yes, I do. In my address book. I sent him a Christmas card for years."

"There ya go," Amelia answered. "If you can get it to me, Michael agreed to keep helping."

Megan eyed her older sister. "Oh, he did, did he?"

Amelia, not one to blush easily, rolled her eyes. "He's become a friend, okay?" Megan thought she noticed a quick look between Amelia and Kate but brushed it off.

"Well if that's settled for now, can we please return to the notebook? Who knows? Maybe Mom outlined the change of hands for us, and we are sitting on the information right here." Megan leaned back in her seat, stretching lazily as her rush of energy started to plateau, earlier than usual. She needed a third cup of coffee or else she'd be napping on the beach while her sisters dug into a treasure trove of juicy family history.

"Right. Let's do it." Kate flipped open the cover, and Clara and Amelia, who were seated on either side of her, instinctively scooted their chairs closer and craned their necks.

Megan pushed air out of her mouth and stood, grabbing a bar stool from the island and propping it behind Kate so she could look over her shoulder.

Their combined silence lasted only a moment.

"The first page was torn out, look," Clara pointed along the jagged edge in the center of the book. After it, a blank page sat.

"Go to the next," Amelia prompted.

Kate turned the page and a new entry materialized. "This is the one that confirmed it was her diary. Look at the date." The oldest pointed at the left corner and read aloud for their benefit.

May 1965

I've never kept a diary. I feel a little silly writing here, but I've got to get this down somewhere and since I'm not allowed to confide in even my own sisters, I will just have to write it here.

No, that won't do. I can't be entirely honest because what if somebody reads this! You can't trust sisters any more than a stranger on the street. They'll share your secrets for little more than a piece of candy. It's true.

And anyway, I'm not entirely sure this is my secret to share. But I just want to put down that there's something going on in my life, and I can't talk about it.

But something I can tell you is that I met someone. Gene. He says he loves me. I can't say I love him back, yet. But he's fun, and he's interested and says he's there for me. I guess that's all you need when you're young and going through something hard.

Well, maybe I'll write here again later if I have time.

Nora

***

"Oh my gosh," Clara whispered. "She sounds like one of my students."

Megan's throat closed up involuntarily. Hearing and seeing her mother's words was at once morbidly fascinating and heart-wrenchingly painful. "What do you think she's talking about? Who's Gene?" Megan asked, swallowing the lump in her throat.

Kate flipped the page. "Let's find out."

Chapter 21—Amelia

They spent the next hour poring over vague entry after vague entry, searching for clues. The name seemed vaguely familiar to Amelia, but she couldn't quite pin it down.

Soon enough, they were burnt out. Every line seemed to hold some suggestion of what the first entry hinted about. Though they didn't get through the whole thing, it was clear that there were wide gaps in when Nora had decided to write—not only because of the chronological expanse between entries but because she'd torn many, many pages out. Perhaps the entries she'd torn out were the most specific ones. The most revealing. Wrought of truth and emotion, like those four she'd left with Michael.

There was no other specific mention of Gene. Yes, some romantic pinings, but each of those did not name anyone, and each felt, well... like it was about a *different* man. Or boy, in the earlier cases.

"Let's take a break," Amelia suggested. "We've learned nothing more than the fact that Mom was a girl with a secret. Lots of secrets, probably."

Clara slid from her seat and took her mug to the sink, rinsing it dutifully. "I agree. I'm ready to hit the beach for a walk or something. It's officially summer. Let's act like it."

Megan checked her wristwatch. "All right. Sounds good to me. We have lots of time before Brian and Sarah get in, and I have nothing to do."

"Well, I have a lot to do," Kate complained, her expression sour. "And I have company coming."

"Company?" Amelia asked, wiggling her eyebrows.

Kate glanced away, clearly suppressing a smile. "Matt is helping me get started on some things around here. I can't wait around to get started. I need income now."

"What about your realty job? And your house? What's the latest on those?" Megan piped up from her squatted position at her bag. She'd been rummaging for a bathing suit, apparently. Of them all, Megan was treating the day like a vacation. It put Amelia in the mood to rent a kayak and head out on the open water.

Holding up her palms and now smiling broadly, Kate confessed, "I quit. And I dropped the price on the house. I'll need to get my furniture out here soon, probably. My old boss said they're expecting to get some nibbles today."

"That's great, Kate," Amelia offered sincerely. She was happy for her older sister. After a lifetime of doing what was expected of her (generally speaking), it was nice to see the Type-A Perfectionist making choices that only *she* wanted to make. In fact, Kate was even more enjoyable to spend time with. Some of her neuroses and anxieties had seemed to subside in favor of a relaxed attitude, generally. Amelia wondered if it wasn't also the reunion with her high school sweetheart that had allowed Kate to loosen up. She hoped so.

"Okay, Kate, you do your thing with Matt. We'll take a break in the sun. Sound good, girls?" Amelia asked, clearing the last of the table into the sink and filling it with hot tap water before squeezing dish soap in.

"Perfect," Clara agreed. Megan nodded, too.

***

As soon as her naked toes curled into the warm sand, Amelia was transported to her youth. Images of herself as a child, building sandcastles with her sisters flooded her brain as Megan and Clara strode ahead toward the marina.

Loud calls from the nearby dock floated across the water and into Heirloom Cove.

Clara turned around ahead, shielding her eyes from the sun with her hand. "Maybe we should walk the other way? Away from the Village?"

Amelia shrugged. "I like walking near the marina." And she did. Amelia loved being in the presence of people—strangers or acquaintances. Friends, too. She missed the friends she'd made in New York and elsewhere. Keeping touch had gotten harder as time passed on. Being around the dock where she hung out as a teenager, made her feel safe.

That was less true for Megan and Clara. Megan wasn't shy, and she probably didn't identify as an introvert, but she could take or leave people. Clara, on the other hand, would be happy as a clam to tuck herself away in a corner of her apartment with a book for hours (if not days) on end.

Still, something in Amelia was drawn toward the harbor, and so she pointed in the opposite direction of where Clara wanted to go. "Let's walk to the Village, get an iced tea to go, then walk back up the shore."

Their sandals dangled in their hands, and the three moved rhythmically across the beach, closer to the boat traffic on the water and foot traffic in town. Tourist season was just beginning to heat up. As a teen, it was Amelia's favorite time of year. It was the time of year she was most likely to find a boyfriend which had often been Amelia's central goal—apart from nailing a main part in the school musical. That dream never did pan out. Once she finally signed up for voice lessons when she was nineteen, the teacher accused her of being tone deaf. *All the grit in the world can't make up for being distinctly unable to carry a tune, young lady. This is why the arts are The Arts! Talent! Chance! You have none!*

It was the harshest advice she'd ever received, and the second most useful. The first most useful came from an acting teacher in Louisville, where she'd spent a spell in hopes of joining their summer stock. That teacher reminded the whole class—all ten of them—that *You don't have to take a class to become an Actor. You just go out there and audition. Simple as that.*

Hah. If only.

Of all the years Amelia had spent chasing her dream, there was only one summer she recalled finding *true* happiness, fleeting though it may have been.

Autumn, just before she moved west, Amelia and her mother and sisters took a girls' trip to Massachusetts. Although Nora, Kate, Amelia, and Clara each wanted to stick to the basics—Boston, New England Clam Chowder, Harvard, Foliage, and so forth, Megan insisted on dragging them to two of her bucket-list locales, as she dubbed them: Salem, the site of Puritanical witch fervor, and Fall River, a tiny, out-of-the-way industrial town that had long ago been home to one of America's most infamous women: Lizzie Borden.

During the Fall River day trip, which was a brief tour of the teetering Victorian house in which Lizzie had been accused of committing patricide, the quirky owner recognized Amelia's flair for memorization and presentation. On the spot, she offered Amelia a summer gig to give tours and help keep up the property.

It was almost a *no*. Amelia planned to be in California the following summer, performing in *Shakespeare in the Park* or taking tickets at the Chinese Theatre, if all else failed.

But Megan had pushed her, literally pushed her, into the cash register where they were purchasing hatchet earrings as souvenirs. "She'd be perfect," Megan promised the woman.

And just like that, Amelia filled out the application and bought a plane ticket to return in May.

Which she did.

It was the best summer of her life.

Had the Borden house not been sold in the following winter, Amelia would have done it again every year until her death. She loved being a docent of the macabre. If she didn't know any better, Amelia would have thought she had a little of Megan's dark spirit living inside of her somewhere.

But it wasn't the ghoulishness of the job that Amelia adored. It was the interacting with guests. Putting on two shows a day. Hosting a captive audience and bringing oddball history to life.

After that summer, her sisters encouraged Amelia to find similar positions in other museums around the country. Or, perhaps she could have worked as a Civil War re-enactor, they implored. But Amelia believed in fate above all else, so when that season of her life had ended, she pressed ahead with her previously scheduled plans.

As Amelia and her sisters neared the dock, she slipped her hand into her front pocket and rubbed her father's watch.

Maybe fate was at it again.

Chapter 22—Kate

"Hi." Kate stood at the door. After her sisters left in their bathing suits and flip-flops, she dashed upstairs and changed into fitted jeans and a relaxed white t-shirt. She'd already blown her hair out that morning and felt that only a quick smear of lip gloss and light coat of mascara would be enough to greet Matt.

She was right. He grinned broadly from the welcome mat. "Hi, Kate."

The moment would be perfect for some affectionate gesture, but she might not execute it well and instead fumble awkwardly through a side hug or force him to kiss her ear instead of her cheek. The smooth thing to do was wait for his lead.

A shared chuckle took the place of their momentary silence. The opportunity passed, and Kate's heart sank a little, but that was okay. They had time.

The plan for that day was for Matt to take measurements for her in the basement and start creating an informal blueprint for her plans to add additional guest rooms. Once they were downstairs, he also offered to help her go through the boxes and bins and move out the furniture. On a whim, she accepted, but mostly because she didn't want him to leave quite yet, even if they would be seeing each other on a more regular basis.

"You don't have another project going on today, do you? I'd hate to keep you from your *real* work," Kate asked as she brought down two tinkling glasses of iced tea. Matt had grabbed a dolly from the bed of his truck and was pulling stacks of boxes from one corner for her to peek into and decide about.

He eased the dolly down, his hand gripping the box on top. "I have to be home by five to cook dinner with Viviana, but otherwise I'm all yours."

Warmth flooded Kate's heart. A man raising a daughter alone tugged at her heart. She wondered how he would have been with Clara. She wondered how he *was* with Viviana. Kate swallowed a lump in her throat. "Tell me about her."

"About Viv?" he replied.

"Yes. I have a sudden urge to know everything about your life."

He grinned and rolled the dolly to a new stack, and Kate realized she'd better start doing her part or they would never get out of that basement. The one where there used to be an old set of sofas, situated around a thin limp rug, board games piled high in the corner between the sofas.

Rolling over another stack of dusty, decaying cardboard, Matt gave her a pointed look. "What about *you*?" he asked. "Tell me about your sons."

Pride flooded Kate. She wasn't the sort of mother to pull out a photo of her handsome boys and flash it in the checkout line at Town and Country, but when given the chance, Kate was liable to talk a man's ear off on the subject. She tried to refrain, but details poured out. Matt listened on as she shared their academic pursuits. Both boys wanted to be engineers like their dad. They eschewed frat life in favor of intra-murals and other on-campus clubs. Ben had a serious girlfriend. They called her every Sunday. She tried not to bug them during the week too much.

"They sound a lot like you," Matt observed when she stopped for a breath.

Kate smiled. "I'd like to think so. I miss them a lot, but I know they're happy. One day, I think they might settle somewhere near here. They claim to be city boys, but we'll see about that." She flipped open the four flaps of a box nearby and peered inside. Mottled, dust-caked afghans. A sigh escaped her mouth. "Keep," she mumbled, drawing a finger toward the side of the staircase they'd designated for Things to be Dealt with Later. "And Viviana? I love her name, by the way."

"It's Italian, if that's not obvious. I had to fight my ex a little. She wanted something white bread and midwestern. Even Vivian would have been a stretch." He chuckled, but Kate knew better than to engage in that particular line of discussion. The laugh fell away, and Matt's expression darkened. "Viv is incredibly smart. Too smart for her own good, if I'm honest."

"I think that's the norm with teenage girls."

"Maybe." He sighed. Instinctively, Kate knew there was a lot more to the story, but she was not bold enough or rude enough to pry.

Licking her lips, she found a response. "With a father like you, I can't imagine she's anything less than perfect."

Grinning again, Matt fixed his gaze on Kate. "You do like me, don't you?"

She flushed and grabbed a dusty throw pillow from the next box she'd opened. "Don't tempt me," she warned, holding it up like a teenager at a sleepover.

Matt pushed his hands forward. "Don't start something you can't finish, Katherine Nora Hannigan."

At that, Kate lowered the pillow. Her lips curled up at the corners. "Actually, Matt," she began, taking a slow step closer to him. "I think we already started this. Thirty years ago."

***

With the basement well underway and an afternoon of innuendo and flirtation (and only one surprising visit from her nosey sisters), Kate and Matt climbed up the stairs and into the kitchen.

Her notepad was flipped open on the island, and as Kate took his glass and hers to the sink, she caught him peek at it.

"Call me a dreamer," she confessed, trying to hide her embarrassment before he could tease her.

He covered for his snooping by shaking his head. "What do you mean?"

Kate indicated the list she had compiled. All the to-dos of setting up a small business. It looked silly when handwritten on lined paper with a pencil like she was some schoolkid. "I'm probably making a huge mistake," she answered half-heartedly.

"I'm lost. A mistake regarding..." he passed his hand between them, and Kate felt her heartbeat double.

"Well that too." Her skin grew warm beneath her t-shirt, and she wondered if he could see the splotchiness climbing up her neck, a dead giveaway for when Kate was overwhelmed with emotion.

Matt licked his lips. "Turning this place into a bed-and-breakfast is a no-brainer. You're smart to do it. You'll need help, though." His voice deepened into a playful warning.

"I can't disagree there." Kate made a mock-serious face, narrowing her eyes and batting her lashes up at him, like a helpless damsel. Then she drew back, playing coy. "It's a good thing I have my sisters for help."

He smirked. "True. I guess you don't need *my* help."

Suddenly, they were standing just inches apart, and Kate had no idea how it happened. Was she floating toward him? Was there some magical magnetism at play? She didn't know. She didn't care. Leaning in, she hooked her hands on his shoulders and raised onto the balls of her feet. Matt lowered himself, gently holding her waist in his hands.

Had he done that ten years ago, she'd have squirmed away. She could stand to lose ten or fifteen pounds, and her body parts weren't the same firm, supple accoutrements that they had been in high school. But Matt's gentle touch and kind, weather-worn face made her feel at once at ease.

Kate pressed her lips to his cheek then whispered, "I don't need you in my life, Matt." He pushed away and stared at her, apparently caught off guard. She giggled before pulling her face back to his, kissing the other cheek and then adding, "I *want* you in my life."

Chapter 23—Clara

"As far as iced tea goes, we can probably get to-go cups from the deli." Clara pointed at the open-air bistro just ahead of them. To the right, incoming boaters shouted jauntily to each other. Speed boats and Ski Dos whizzed across the water, adding more noise to an already busy Village. Clara had always liked the *idea* of Birch Village more than she liked *being* at Birch Village. She wasn't about to have a panic attack or anything. She could handle it. But lots of people and loud places drained her of energy rather than engorging her with it, like was true of Amelia, who subconsciously began humming and walking with a little rhythm ahead of Megan and Clara.

"Is she dancing?" Megan stage-whispered to Clara. "I think she's dancing."

Clara just smiled and shook her head. "Yes, she's dancing." Clara shrank back a step from her sisters, neither of whom minded the attention. They turned and laughed at her before falling into the easy beat of the busy tourist station. A crowd of bikini-clad teenagers cut between Clara and her sisters, forcing her to fall farther behind.

"Miss Hannigan?" One of the girls pulled down her Ray-Bans, her jaw falling open at the sight of a teacher outside of the classroom. Always an odd situation both for Clara and for the students in question.

"Girls, hello!" she cheered, noting the jarring lack of fabric that the fourteen-year-olds were walking around in. She tried to reserve judgment, recalling that peer pressure sank its teeth deep.

The group each giggled awkwardly, taking turns in saying hi. She knew all of them except for one, a taller, blonder, tanner version than her students. And, though Clara wasn't in the position to classify pubescents based on their objective beauty, well, the unfamiliar girl was markedly prettier. As pretty as Mercy, the poor outsider who hadn't quite harnessed her potential. Perhaps, she never would. Clara smiled at the beachy bombshell, trying to hide her awe at just how intimidating children could be.

It was no wonder Mercy was afraid of high school.

Clara would be too.

***

"Miss Hannigan?"

Just as Clara was about to catch up to her sisters, a second, deeper voice called out to her, mimicking the earlier one from the precocious promoted eighth grade crew.

Turning her head toward the dock and the source of the greeting, Clara winced when she identified it.

Jake Hennings.

"Mr. Hennings!" Clara replied, her voice a little louder and a little higher than it would be normally. She glanced quickly back at the group of girls who'd just passed by. Was Mercy with them? Confusion clouded her thought process, and she looked back at him and frowned.

"It's Jake, remember?"

Smiling now, she hooked a thumb at the group of girls. "Are you chaperoning Mercy and..." The word *friends* caught in Clara's throat, and a flicker shone in Mr. Hennings'—or, *Jake's*—eyes. She shook her head and began to backpedal, as though she'd almost endured a faux pas, but he read her mind.

"Oh, those girls? Are they in Mercy's class?"

It was a loaded question, Clara realized. He was at once asking if the prematurely beautiful and buoyant young ladies were the same age as his own socially disinterested and waifish daughter. And, if they were, that fact could cast a glare on Mercy's status as a loner.

Then again, Clara could be projecting. She swallowed her worries and smiled brightly. "Some of them are in her grade, yes." She glanced at his t-shirt, which bore a pinned nametag, then looked beyond him to the dock. "Are you... *working*?"

He scratched the back of his head and followed her gaze. "Yeah. I manage the marina." He waved a hand around, but it wasn't a gesture of embarrassment. It wasn't one of pride, either. Jake wasn't aware that Clara knew a great deal about him. He wasn't a dock jockey or a boat boy. Jake Hennings was a professor and a researcher. He was educated, and though he didn't put on airs of sophistication or the like, he oozed self-assurance and intellect. Confidence and calm and cleverness and perhaps even bookishness. The job wasn't a fit. She could see that as plain as day. Yet, there he was, happy as a clam. Jake Hennings was more than her student's handsome father.

To Clara, he was a charming enigma. Something—some*one*—who might work into her daydreams and thoughts. A summer crush, even. Her legs began to feel rubbery beneath her weight. "I'd better let you get back to work," she said, her voice trembling.

If she didn't know any better, she'd have said a shadow of disappointment crossed his face.

"Tell Mercy I said hello!" Clara added, offering him a final smile before striding off toward the deli. When she got there, she looked behind to see if she could spot Jake among the crowd. Maybe he was still looking at her.

But he wasn't. A new group of bikini-clad bodies had taken Clara's place. This set was an older one. College-aged girls, perhaps. He was pointing toward the dock, obviously giving them directions they definitely did not need.

***

"So, what's the next step, here?" Clara asked Amelia as they crossed back toward the beach after all three had gotten their drinks. She kept an eye out for Jake, but he was nowhere to be seen. He probably took off on a cruise around the lake with some gorgeous tourist. That's how it went in Birch Harbor. Tourists became as appealing to lonely locals as Birch Harbor was to destination-craving tourists. Maybe he'd already learned that.

"What do you mean?" Amelia smiled broadly to an unfamiliar group of people who'd just descended from the dock and were looking around as if to pin down a tour guide or something.

"Do you know them?" Megan asked.

Amelia pointed. "Yes. That's Mr. Carmichael. Don't you remember? Our old principal. He looks lost."

Clara looked over her shoulder. The group who received Amelia's wave did seem confused and lost, in fact, and the man leading the way did not look familiar at all, but of course he wouldn't have been Clara's principal. "I don't think he recognizes you," she pointed out impatiently, ready to move off the marina and onto the cove.

"True," Amelia admitted, coming to a complete stop. She raised her hand to shield her eyes from the sun and called past Clara to the strangers. "Mr. Carmichael?"

"Nooo," Clara hissed beneath her breath. She hated that sort of thing. Her mother did it all the time, stopping to talk to strangers and acquaintances alike. It drove Clara nuts. The conversations were never ending. Twenty minutes in, Clara would have to make the decision to either extricate herself from the situation and wait elsewhere, to avoid a total panic attack, or rudely interrupt to remind her mother they had somewhere to be.

Megan sighed too. "Amelia," she said under her breath, "make it fast. I'm not in the mood to rehash past suspensions."

"Yes?" the older gentleman in a Hawaiian shirt and white shorts said to Amelia, his face the color of paper beneath a wide-brimmed straw hat.

"You might remember us," Amelia replied, passing her hand between Megan and herself. Clara shrank in embarrassment. He clearly did *not* remember them.

Still, the man smiled unsteadily and nodded his head. "Let me guess. Former students, no doubt?"

"That's right!" Amelia appeared to glow. It occurred to Clara that being recognized was an important thing to her older sister. "Amelia Hannigan. And this is Megan Hannigan." She continued to babble for a few moments, sharing the year they graduated and a silly memory about some school play gone wrong. As she did, Clara watched a spark catch in the old man's eyes as the others in his group grew bored.

"Hannigan," he said once Amelia stopped to take a breath.

"That's right, sir."

To Clara's surprise, he reared back a step then slowly looked over his left shoulder toward the house on the harbor. "Nora Hannigan. You—" A deep frown furrowed his eyebrows and set him back a second step.

But Amelia just smiled. "Yes, Nora's our mother. You probably know her. Or, *knew* her, I mean."

He stood a little taller and turned to the woman at his elbow. "Of course," he said to her and the others who began meandering behind him. "Nora Hannigan." He turned back to Amelia. "Your mother and I went to school together. A long time ago. I do remember you girls." A crooked grin shaped his mouth, distorting his features as a gold molar flashed in the far corner.

Clara narrowed her eyes on him, a sense of foreboding sweeping beneath her skin.

The woman to Mr. Carmichael's right side wrapped a papery hand around his arm and leaned into him. "We have lunch reservations, sweetheart."

He turned in a choppy circle, his travel mates following his unsteady gaze over to the Village, "My wife and I moved inland years ago, but we brought some friends for an overnight trip," he gestured behind him to the row of vessels, each nestled in its mooring.

Clara followed his wave, her gaze seizing a modest houseboat. The name on the side of it caught her attention. *Harbor Hawk*. The school mascot was the hawk. Made sense.

Megan cleared her throat behind Clara, urging the conversation to wrap up, but Amelia couldn't help but to pipe up one more time.

"Are you staying on your boat?" Her eyes grew wide, and she threw a look to Clara and Megan. Clara felt nausea rise up in her throat.

Mr. Carmichael's wife and group now detached themselves from him and moved off the path and to the wooden planks of the plaza. He stuck his hands in his shorts and jangled them a little. "Yes." His smile left his eyes but lingered on his puffy mouth. Clara inhaled sharply, about to pull Amelia away and save them all.

"Well if you decide you'd rather sleep on dry land," Amelia began, her eyes brightening and one hand flashing up like she was starring in a commercial, "our oldest sister, Kate—you might remember her? She graduated a couple years ahead of me?" Amelia left out a big detail there. "She's converting our house,"—Amelia pointed clearly at the Inn just next to the harbor—"into a bed-and-breakfast. I bet she'd be thrilled if you and your group wanted to test it out."

Clara squeezed her eyes shut and shrank away, officially turning and taking a few casual steps away from her embarrassing sister. Kate would be absolutely *mortified* if she had to scramble to set up for her old *principal*, of all people. And Clara didn't find him to be the sort of person she or anyone would want to make special accommodations for. Why Amelia was so happy to throw him a bone was beyond her. He seemed like a smarmy tourist. And a houseboat? What school principal owned a houseboat?

Turning to assess the situation, Clara caught Megan's eye and they exchanged a silent agreement. Clara strode back just as Megan took a cue and spoke up. "We've got to be going, but how about we take your phone number and let you know if Kate has a vacancy this evening?"

The man's face fell, and Amelia glared at Megan then Clara. "I'm sure she does. They don't want to spend the night on a boat." Amelia jutted her chin out down the dock. "Even if it's a *house*boat."

He grinned. "I'd love to stay at your sister's bed-and-breakfast. Maybe another time. We could have a Birch Harbor High reunion. Have I got stories about your mother." His voice softened, and he stared off toward the house. "Say," he went on as his wife returned, probably to forcibly extract him from Amelia's affable grasp. "I heard about your father. Please accept my condolences."

The three of the sisters were stunned into silence.

Finally, Megan spoke up. "You must mean our *mother*," she pointed out.

Confusion spread across his face. "Your *mother*?"

His wife tugged his arm. "The others are waiting for us, dear."

"She passed at the end of last month," Clara murmured, studying his reaction.

He passed a hand over his mouth, his expression entirely somber. "I'm terribly sorry to hear it."

Amelia, Megan, and Clara now stood silent. Even Amelia came to her senses enough to let the poor, confused man be on his way.

"Oh, girls," the wife said, once Mr. Carmichael broke from his odd reverie and started to turn. "Do you know if there's a Visitor Center or a place we can get some information about local attractions?"

Amelia raised her eyebrows and looked at her youngest sister. "Clara? Do you know anything about that?"

Clara had never once played tour guide. She could direct them around the Village and up toward the school and any other main locale, but her mind was turning a blank. "Um," she began. "We *used* to have a museum..." It was the best she could offer.

"A museum sounds lovely," the lady replied earnestly.

Amelia replied, "I'm sorry, I think my little sister is right. Birch Harbor doesn't have a museum anymore. Maybe if you go to the marina office, they can give you more information about local sightseeing. As far as I know, it's the marina and the lake that people come for." She smiled sweetly, and the woman thanked them again, finally wandering off as Mr. Carmichael lifted his hand in a weak wave. "Nice to see you, girls."

The three of them mirrored his wave, muttering low goodbyes as his wife tugged him gently in the direction of Fiorillo's. "Come on, Gene. Let's find the others."

***

"That was weird," Clara observed once Mr. Carmichael and his wife were out of earshot.

Amelia shrugged. "Memory gets weird when you're old. Everyone was sort of amazed when Dad left. It was a bit of a town scandal, ironically."

"Ironically?"

"Well, Mom thought Kate's pregnancy would doom her reputation. In fact, it was Dad's departure, clearly." Amelia passed a hand back toward the confused former principal. "It was even Mr. Carmichael's most vivid recollection, clearly."

"I don't know about that," Megan lifted her eyebrow. "Seems like he remembered Mom pretty well." She grinned and together Amelia and Megan seemed to shrug off the whole exchange.

Clara let it go. It occurred to her that Birch Harbor history was a tapestry of personal connections and bizarre remembrances. It wasn't the first time someone apologized about Wendell Acton's absence. And she had better get used to people doing the same for Nora now.

"Where *do* tourists go when they come to town?" Megan asked once the trio had made it down a sandy set of wooden steps and onto the beach, their iced teas sweating in the late morning warmth.

Clara took a long drink from her iced tea then came up for air. It was funny that she possessed some knowledge her older sisters didn't have. She felt a little like a gatekeeper, even in the wake of being left out of the reunion with Principal Carmichael. "I have no idea. Mom was always involved in that sort of thing, though. You'd have thought she was Birch Harbor's official greeter. But she always dragged her guests and visitors to the country club or church. Or here," Clara waved back toward the Village.

"What kinds of visitors did Mom have?" Megan asked, throwing Clara a sidelong glance.

A laugh escaped Clara's mouth. "All kinds," she answered. "I mean, *you* know."

"Not really," Megan answered.

Clara looked at Amelia for confirmation from the oldest among them. Amelia nodded her on, granting permission to dish out details. "You have a special insight into the secret life of Nora Hannigan, babe," Amelia said, lowering her drink and pulling her sunglasses from her head onto her nose.

"What are you *talking* about?" Clara asked.

"Girl," Amelia answered, "We had Nora as a typical mom. Flighty, sure. Distracted, yes. And of course, she had already begun her country club nights and church commitments, but by the time we were out of the house, it was just beginning."

"*What* was just beginning?" Clara asked lamely.

"Her midlife crisis," Megan answered, her voice flat.

"Oh." Clara considered this. It was obvious she had grown up with a woman who hadn't expected to raise a child well into her golden years. But there were no secrets. No scandals. None that Clara was aware of, at least.

But Megan and Amelia seemed to disagree.

Chapter 24—Megan

Megan slurped the bottom of her plastic cup through a straw and searched the beach for a trash can, forgetting momentarily that most of the shoreline was semi-private land.

They'd walked four houses south of the house on the harbor. Kate's so-called *Inn*. Megan quelled a little bit of envy at the thought. It wasn't so much *envy* as it was pride, truly. She was proud of her big sister for finding a place in the world. And, Megan genuinely wanted to help. Then there was her little sister with security in her teaching position.

Sometimes, Megan felt like she and Amelia were a pair of middle-child misfits, roaming the earth with no direction. In comparison to Kate and Clara, they really were.

Of course, none of that was the reason Megan longed for a career. By and large, she had enjoyed being a homemaker and raising Sarah with Brian. Their life was good. It was only in the last couple years that a bit of cabin fever had set in. Restlessness. An urge to get the ball rolling on her own life. While Megan was far less of a dreamer than any of her three sisters, she just couldn't shake the itch that there was a job out there with her name on it. Specifically, a boutique matchmaking service.

As they strolled the beach now, new ideas formed in her brain. Secret ideas. She had a running list of ways she would magically put together a little business (kind of like Kate was doing). Maybe she'd drop a flyer at various eateries in her hometown: *Need a date? Call Megan!*

That would send the wrong message.

Maybe she could get business cards made and fake it a little. *Here, I have a little matchmaking business. Call me if you're in the market. Or rather...* on *the market*, she could say with a wink as she passed over an eggshell-white card.

In her reveries, Megan was making the rounds out in the suburbs, among housewives and professionals who were already paired off. It made no sense. Matchmaking in Suburbia would never bring in business.

Not that it was *business* that Megan wanted.

It was connections. Or, rather, *connecting*. That was her *thing*. No, she was not Amelia, flamboyant and bubbly. And, she wasn't Kate, composed and professional but dutifully extroverted.

She was *Megan*. Enigmatic, hopefully. Interesting. Complicated and complex and surprisingly fascinated by human behavior and the concept of soul mates.

It dawned on her that maybe her quirkiness had to do with her own history of romance. High school boyfriends every week. Fly-by-night success with dating in the earliest days of college. Until she met studious Brian in her dorm. They'd bumped into each other (literally) one night in the halls. He was heading back to his room from a study session with friends. She had left a party early (parties weren't exactly Megan's style). It was curious that they hadn't run into each other in the weeks before, since their rooms were just a few hallways apart.

But there they were, maimed and gobsmacked to face each other so viscerally. He'd apologized over and again, and she drank it all up. Just as they were about to go their separate ways, he turned and asked if he could have her dorm room number.

Without a second thought she gave it to him, and well, their love affair began. A slow, taunting affair in which Megan insisted on upholding her Catholic values. An affair of nonstop kissing until they made it to the altar not long thereafter. The kissing eventually slowed down, especially once Sarah was born. But the flame of their affection had only begun to weaken in the past year or so. Ever since Megan spoke about her desires to really get into the workforce. To strike out on her own.

What in the *world* was Brian afraid of? That he'd lose her?

No.

That wasn't his style. Brian and Megan's relationship was built on a solid foundation of mutual trust. Respect, too, or so she had thought.

All she could point to was his anxiety over money. For the entirety of their marriage and in the months and years before, Brian feared they'd be destitute. Megan couldn't quite relate. Coming from a long line of people who worked their butts off and living in an ancestral home on the banks of Lake Huron, for all it wasn't, ensured Megan had a strong sense of financial security. Worst case scenario? She could work.

But Brian's background was markedly different. His parents weren't the work-hard-play-hard types. His mother stayed at home, nervously cooking meals of Ramen and potatoes, while his father hopped around to different jobs, never satisfied with his boss or working conditions. Money was scarce for Brian and his siblings. They weren't certain they'd pay the bills.

Brian wanted this certainty in life, Megan knew. Maybe he didn't trust her to actually help in that regard.

Her nostrils flared at this realization now, as they came to a stop where the beach sand was cut off by a sharp outcropping of rocks.

Amelia walked ahead and stepped up onto a boulder, balancing gracefully. "Remember when we used to come here to look for tadpoles?" she asked, her arms spread out like she owned the town.

Megan grinned at the memory. Forever, she had been the youngest of three, scrambling after her two big sisters on various adventures along the beach, nearly drowning or cracking her head open on multiple occasions. Kate would always fret over whether to call an ambulance or, worst case, Mom. Amelia would always hush them both and convince Megan that A. she was *fine*! And B. it was her fault *anyway*!

"That's the one thing Mom was good at," Megan mused.

Amelia jumped down and kicked sand out to the water. "What do you mean?"

"She just let us be kids, you know? Not like parents today. Certainly not like Brian and me."

"You never let Sarah go out and play?"

"We did, but you know how it is. Times are different. The world is a scarier place," Megan replied, her low voice lost to the humid air.

"I think," Amelia began, "that the world is the same. It's no scarier now than it was before. It's just us. We're more scared. Less busy. More fearful."

Megan just shrugged. She wasn't going to argue with someone who didn't have kids. Amelia couldn't understand.

Amelia kicked another spray of sand into the lake then followed it, walking into the shallow water. Clara and Megan instinctively followed her, each testing the water first. Megan pressed her feet into the wet sand that spanned a couple feet to the waterline, digging her toes into it as deep as they would go. It was like a little beach-style massage, grinding her skin against the warm grains. The water was nice enough, for early summer, and she ventured after Clara, who now stood in the lake, the water lapping up against her shins by then.

Amelia stood farther out and deeper in, bending every few moments to dip her hands in the water and splash it out away from the shore.

Megan took a step closer to Clara, her long, gossamer sarong sticking to the skin beneath her knees where it had grown wet.

Amelia wore a tankini top and cut-off jean shorts that were short enough to belong on a teenager instead of a woman north of forty. But the girl could pull it off. Her legs were long and toned. Megan also had their father's long legs, and she thought they were pretty defined. It was one of the perks of being at home, lots of opportunity for yoga and Pilates. Lots of long walks. Still, the difference between Amelia, the carefree dreamer with the body of a would-be actress, and Megan, the repressed homemaker with a teenage daughter and a looming divorce, was easy to spot. One had her whole life before her, still. The other had her whole life behind her.

Megan kicked at the water, sending a spray just to the right of Amelia, spritzing her.

"Hey!" Amelia shrieked. "What's the big idea?" She feigned a Bronx accent and reared her leg back, threatening to splash Megan in revenge.

Megan squealed and high-kneed behind Clara just in time for Amelia to bend over and send two handfuls of lake water in their direction.

Clara screamed, too, and together she and Megan ran hand-in-hand to the shore, just a few feet away.

Laughter brought them to their knees in the sand, Megan's sarong now drenched. Amelia joined them, falling to the beach in her wet jean shorts and slick swimsuit top.

"We should have brought a picnic," Amelia declared.

"We can always grab lunch back at the Village," Clara suggested. Megan saw that she had come to life a bit. If only Kate were there, too, and they'd be outright bonding.

"Do either of you have your phone?" Megan asked. She'd left hers behind, which was probably a bad idea, since she was expecting a phone call that afternoon. But they wouldn't be out too long.

"I do." Amelia tugged her device loose from her front pocket. "It's after twelve already."

"Call Kate and see if she wants to meet us for a burger or something."

After no answer from their fearless leader, the trio decided to walk back to the harbor and get their own lunch. After all, it was clear Kate had other priorities, and who were her sisters to get in the way of that?

Once they'd been walking quietly for a few minutes, Clara spoke up. "What was Mom like before I came along?"

"What do you mean?" Megan asked, retying her sarong for the twentieth time.

"I feel like there is a huge divide," Clara answered, her tone more somber.

"Of course there is," Megan answered, clicking her tongue. "You're a lot younger than us."

"You were a toddler when I moved out," Amelia added. "Despite the whole 'adoption' thing," Amelia drew air quotes, "it was like we had a little baby girl, not a baby sister."

Clara laughed without mirth. "I guess a four-year-old isn't sister material to teenagers."

Megan and Amelia exchanged a nervous glance over Clara's floppy sun hat. Megan took the reins. "You were a little princess. You didn't have to be our sister, you know? It was kind of better that you weren't, probably. Otherwise Amelia might have talked you into something dangerous. You could have died if you were any older, actually."

The three of them laughed at the joke, but it was clear Clara was asking something that neither Megan nor Amelia had the answer for.

Still, Megan made an effort. "What was Mom like before you were born? That's the question?"

Amelia's pace slowed as she added, "Or do you mean what was Mom like before Kate got pregnant?"

Silence took over as all three of them slowed to a stop. They were halfway between two shore-side houses now, in a public slice of the beach with a little walkway that ran up to the street.

Megan laughed at Amelia's point, but Clara didn't. She frowned and stared off at the water. "Was it that bad?" the youngest of the three asked, her voice trembling.

"No," Amelia answered immediately, slinging an arm around Clara and making a pointed face at Megan, who jumped in.

"Actually," Megan went on. "For *you* it was great. Weirdly great."

"What do you mean?" Clara cocked her head.

"When they decided that Mom would adopt you, it sort of... it helped her refocus, I think." Megan, too, was staring across the rippling water. The sun above them took on an oven effect, and Megan felt a line of sweat form along her spine.

"Refocus? You mean because Wendell left?" Clara was no stranger to the conversation, but it made sense if she still acted a little out of the loop. After all, she *was*.

"'Left,' yeah." Megan answered, arching one eyebrow to Amelia who shook her head.

Clara shrugged Amelia's arm off her shoulder. "Okay, out with it," she demanded, anger reddening her face. "You two are always doing this. Making these little innuendos back and forth about some scandalous past that I used to be too young to know. Well, I'm not too young anymore." Her blonde ponytail bounced as she shoved her arms across her chest, crossing them there with a purpose.

Megan's jaw fell open a bit at the display of ire. Fair point to Clara. She deserved to know.

Even if all they had to share was mere speculation.

Chapter 25—Amelia

"Listen, Clara." Amelia turned and faced her little sister, gripping the girl's delicate shoulders firmly. "We don't think Dad *left* us."

Her blue eyes grew wide. "You think Mom—*Nora*—left *him*?"

Megan sighed and shook her head. "No. They were madly in love. It was a volatile love affair, theirs."

"How so?" Clara's face fell back into a skeptical expression, but she uncrossed her arms. In tandem, the three resumed their slow walk back along the cove and toward the harbor.

"They fought, and they made up all the time. I think Mom's mood swings hit an all-time high when we were teenagers. But Dad knew how to bring her back down to earth without placating her or excusing her behavior. Still, he was no pushover. When they fought, you could hear it clear up to the lighthouse. It's no wonder that's where he went when we went to Arizona."

"About that," Clara interrupted. "Why go? Why not just stay here and lie low?"

"Mom wanted to hide Kate, and it would be suspicious if Megan and I were roaming around town without our big sister. We went *everywhere* together, and Mom wasn't stupid."

"But why was she *so* mortified? Teenage pregnancy isn't *that* rare," Clara argued, sucking down the dregs of her by-now watered-down tea.

"In 1992, teen pregnancy was still a scandal. I mean it still is, *right*?" It was Megan who spoke this time. Ever the realist.

"And besides," Amelia added more softly. "We sort of had a reputation to uphold."

"What reputation?" Clara asked.

"Mom and Dad had just gotten situated with The Bungalows. They had joined the country club. Things were going well for them financially. Better than they ever had, actually. Mom couldn't stand to lose that, you know?"

Clara seemed to mull it over. "She saw herself as a glamor girl?"

"I wouldn't say that," Amelia answered, deep in thought. "She was gritty, you know? She didn't mind if anyone saw her with a little dirt beneath her fingernails. She was happy for people to see her helping Dad carry a defunct toilet to the barn, water splashing on her overalls." Amelia and Megan laughed together at the memory, but Clara didn't know it.

"She wasn't embarrassed by any of that, but she was embarrassed that Kate got pregnant?"

Amelia glanced at Clara. "I think it was a combination of factors. When Kate got pregnant, it haunted Mom. She went quiet on us. And on Dad. He thought Kate could raise you, you know."

"He did?"

"Oh yeah," Megan joined in. "He thought everything could stay the same and that we'd just grow into this big happy family."

"So, they disagreed?" Clara wondered aloud.

"Definitely. The whole mess was why it was easy for Mom to tell us that he left. She knew that we knew they were at odds over the decision." Megan kicked a mound of sand from her path as she recounted the same thing Amelia knew to be true.

Clara slowed. "So why did Mom disagree? Just because she didn't want her teenage daughter to be a young mother?"

"It was deeper than that. More... *personal*," Megan replied. Amelia shot her a look.

"You think?" Amelia asked now, surprised at Megan's insight.

They walked farther north along the lake while the sun reached its peak high above them and leisurely began its lazy summer descent.

"I'm already hungry," Amelia complained. "Should we grab a seat at the Village?"

"I'm not in the mood for Italian," Megan replied.

"What about the deli?" Amelia suggested.

Clara shook her head. "There's a new place there we could try. Green Birch Bistro."

***

Green Birch Bistro was a perfect lunch spot if ever there was one. And if the setting didn't prove as much, the long wait certainly did. But the sisters had nowhere to be, at least not at that moment, and so they accepted a plastic buzzer and took the hostess's advice to stroll down to the lake, a short jaunt from the restaurant's patio.

"How did we not know about this place? It's great." It occurred to Amelia that she had some exploring to do. Her hometown had changed more than *she* had.

Soon enough, the sisters were seated on a quaint, quasi-private patio, which jutted from the back of the restaurant onto a narrow deck that hovered past the sea wall, encroaching on the beach by some yards.

Amelia figured it was as good a time as any to get back to solving the family mystery. She hadn't heard from Michael yet, who had appointments that morning but promised to use his spare time for digging around, but Amelia could at least dig through the recesses of her memory and even pull in her sisters, who might help alight on a clue they'd previously overlooked.

Once their drinks were served, she pulled the watch from her pocket and laid it out in the center of the table. "That," Amelia pointed to it, "is what Mom left me in the will. Remember?"

Megan and Clara nodded, and Megan said, "Yes." But their blank looks suggested they were not thinking what Amelia was.

"Why would she include it in the will if she didn't *have* it?" Amelia took a blue packet from the sweetener dish, tore it, and tapped it into her iced tea, stirring ruthlessly. All the coffee and tea in the world wouldn't help her with the family puzzle, and surely she'd regret the caffeine buzz come evening when it was time to quiet her mind, but for now she needed every little bit of energy she could borrow. The problem of where their dad went was starting to feel somehow relevant. Crucial. Urgent, even. Though Amelia didn't know why.

"Maybe she thought she had it," Clara offered, shrugging and pulling her lemon wedge from the lip of her glass before setting it on the table.

"I'll take that." Amelia reached across and plucked the slice of citrus, squeezing it into her glass. "Good point, Clara."

"No way," Megan inserted. She stared across at the water, a darkness falling across her features. "Even if Mom was losing it, she knew *exactly* what she had possession of and exactly what she did *not* have possession of."

Amelia frowned. "That's quite an assumption."

"No. It's reality. Kate and I discussed the will last weekend when she was going through the garden shed. In the paperwork Michael read to us, Mom left Kate twenty-three flowerpots. *Twenty-three*. She wrote that thing years ago, so why be so specific?"

"Did Kate find twenty-three flowerpots?" Amelia asked, unused to being the skeptic of the group.

Megan simply grinned. "Exactly."

"What about everything else in there?" Clara asked.

Amelia took a long swig of her tea. "What do you mean?"

"Have each of you claimed the things she left you?" Sadness peeked through Clara's innocent question. The hurt of her exclusion from the will, no doubt. Amelia wanted to wrap the little blonde in a big blanket, carry her to the house on the harbor and give it all to her. None of those silly possessions mattered to Amelia. She wasn't the sort to keep mementos, not like Kate or Clara, who could have everything if they wanted it. Amelia was happy to be in charge of running The Bungalows or having a job to do. She was a doer more than a keeper. That was Amelia.

"No," Megan answered on both their behalf.

Clara was about to take a sip, but stopped, awkwardly extracting the straw from her mouth before protesting. "So, we are more concerned with the properties we got and less concerned with the... what, the *trinkets* from the estate?" If Amelia didn't know better, she'd say a look of modest disgust crossed Clara's face.

She glanced at Megan, who must have shared her offense, because Megan replied, "It's not like we *forgot*."

Lifting an eyebrow, Clara returned her straw to her mouth and took a long pull of water. She seemed to ignore Megan's defensive response.

Amelia let out a long sigh. "It's something we need to do, no doubt. And we *will*. But Mom didn't only leave Dad's wristwatch." She picked up the hardware and turned it in her hand, amazed at its condition.

"That's true. She left me his wedding band." Megan's eyes flashed at Amelia. "Wait a minute."

A chill ran up Amelia's spine, sending goosebumps along her arms. "Oh, my Lord."

The food came, a brief but obnoxious interruption. Amelia feigned appreciation, but as soon as the waiter left, she pressed her hands on the top of the table dramatically.

Megan didn't touch her food. Clara's face crumpled into confusion. "What am I missing?" the latter asked.

"Mom wrote the will after *you* were born. We *know* that. And if it was after you were born, then obviously it was after Dad disappeared."

"Left the picture you mean?" Clara added.

"*Disappeared*," Megan corrected.

The conversation was heating up, and Clara was about to be left out if she didn't get on board. Amelia spoke directly to her now. "Clara, if Mom wrote that will knowing that Dad was gone, then why in the *world* would she leave Megan his wedding band?"

Megan's face fell. "He must have left it behind."

Chapter 26—Clara

"He might have," Clara answered weakly. She had no idea if the wedding band was still on their father's finger, wherever he was, or what.

But she had a head start on looking. Clara had searched high and low for her mother's hope chest. She was *still* searching. She'd scoured every box and nook and cranny in the house on the harbor. The *Inn*. And by now she was over halfway through the cottage. Each night, she committed no less than an hour to the hunt for that hope chest. If the wedding ring was still in Birch Harbor somewhere, that's where it would be. "How come you didn't think of this when we were in Michael's office?" Clara asked.

"Distracted? Confused? Grief-ridden? Take your pick, Kid," Amelia spat back.

Clara rolled her eyes. When Amelia's attitude came out, she wanted to crawl under a rock and disappear. For such a magnetic personality, the woman could be as sassy and condescending as she was enthusiastic and charming.

"How do you know he didn't leave it behind?" Megan pressed in reply, her mouth full of salad.

"I lived with Mom, remember? We went through her jewelry boxes right after her diagnosis. It wasn't there."

Amelia scoffed. "That doesn't mean she wasn't keeping it somewhere, right?"

Shrugging, Clara bit into a chicken tender.

The feeling of being wrong about it nagged in her brain as Amelia droned on with wild theories about some father who didn't walk out on them, hiding for good, but was forced out.

"What?" Clara asked after Amelia's last suggestion. "You think Mom... you think *Nora Hannigan* kicked him out?"

The brunette nodded somberly. "Like I said... theirs was a *passionate* marriage."

"You've been watching too many soap operas." Megan stretched back in her chair.

Amelia protested. "There's no telling how angry she was when he disagreed with her about Clara."

Though Clara had never met Wendell Acton and generally agreed with her sisters that he must have been something of a flake to disappear without a trace. But that's just it. Such a kind-natured sort of man wouldn't up and leave.

Maybe Nora Hannigan was awful enough to push him away.

Dread washed over Clara.

Or maybe... worse.

The rest of lunch was a quiet, tense affair. None of them spoke what was on her mind, but Clara had the distinct sense that they shared the same suspicion, at least to a degree.

They split the check three ways and began the short walk home.

As the three sisters moved through the wooden slats of the Village walkways, Clara scanned the harbor for signs of Jake. She was curious about his new job there. It was a far cry from what Mercy said he did when he worked at the university. From college professor to marina manager? Well, maybe not *so* far a cry. He had studied Lake Huron, after all. Now he was living there. It could work. Her stomach churned with discontent about how the first day of summer was unfolding.

Too many questions.

Not enough answers.

And Clara didn't even want any—of either. She was officially on vacation. She could use a break from the whole process of inquiry and study and *work*. She wanted to get down to moving out of the apartment and *into* the cottage. That was her priority now. Not searching for Wendell Acton. Not renovating the house she'd cleaned all her life. Clara needed distance from sisters.

She needed a *friend*.

Chapter 27—Megan

A detour to The Bungalows was in order. Amelia announced to Megan and Clara that she wanted to check on her *assets,* as she'd taken to calling the small complex of individual, ground-level units. After the recent reading of the will, Megan had expected Amelia to jump on the project with fervor, maybe choosing a new color to paint the shabby wood siding.

Instead, she'd set her sights elsewhere, clearly.

Since she'd seen to her duty of learning that their mom's personal diary was little more than a hodgepodge collection of teenage ramblings (though the torn out entries certainly intrigued Megan), the third Hannigan sister now only had to wait for Brian and Sarah to show up for their reunion at the cemetery.

She wondered if he'd want to grab dinner after or if his whole visit really was just to offer respects to Nora. Megan didn't care if he left after. That would suit her fine. She could get Sarah set up with Clara then tuck herself in for an early bedtime. Lots of sleep. That would do her good.

Kate had been downstairs, rummaging through boxes with Matt when they barged into the house and so Megan and the others decided to leave them be.

Megan left it up to her and Clara to coordinate an arrangement for the older party who'd been wandering around town.

She couldn't fathom being in Kate's shoes, single and flirting with the idea of *getting back out there*, as well-meaning couples often pushed. Having married Brian so young, Megan's dating life was non-existent. She didn't know what it meant to travel alone. Maybe people enjoyed the option to see what they wanted to see and do what they wanted to do. Megan could appreciate that. The freedom. But then what about at night? In a foreign hotel room or a cozy bed-and-breakfast? Did they lie awake thinking how nice it would be to snuggle against someone's chest and recount the day's events?

That's what Megan loved about their family vacations. Sarah would be tucked into her own bed just feet away, and Brian and Megan would whisper about how wonderful a trip it was. How lucky they were. What a charmed life they led.

Family vacations were a point of pride for the couple. Or at least, they *had* been. Brian, who loathed traveling, would take every measure to ensure a perfect trip, including saving as much as possible in the intervening years. To both ends, the Stevensons only went away together a rash of times in the past two decades. But each vacation was a blow out. First-class tickets gave way to private cars with concierge service at the hotel. Lately, Megan wondered if Brian put out money to see to his own comfort. If he could alleviate stress for himself, he'd be more enjoyable for Megan and Sarah. That was her cynical impression on the situation.

Though, it didn't jibe with the man she'd married. The frugal penny-pincher who'd just as soon never go *anywhere* if he could get away with it.

Perhaps the extravagant vacations were more about his wife and daughter after all. They were the one thing in her marriage—in her *life*—that she cherished. She bragged about. Looked forward to. He knew that and clung to it, sharing in the storytelling for months and years after each trip. Showing off photos to his coworkers. Reflecting with Megan on the sofa or in bed late at night about how *perfect* their life was. How *lucky* they were.

They hadn't been on vacation in a couple of years now. No projects, either. They didn't really have anything in their marriage to look forward to. Save, perhaps, for Sarah's impending flight out of the house and to college.

That might have been something to rejoice over, for more reasons than one. It could be an opportunity for Megan to get back in the workforce.

Brian's financial fears would have to have taken a backseat at one point. There was no room for happiness in a life built on fear. And that was Brian. A fearful, worrisome man who was more concerned with basic survival than he was with day-to-day joys. Of course, until he worked up the energy (and built a savings) to let loose every few years. Those were the golden moments. Megan often wondered if she could just freeze Brian in those times—when he had the money and emotional freedom to splurge on a vacation—maybe things would not have crumbled into boredom.

Maybe it wouldn't have come to divorce.

Maybe it still didn't have to.

Megan's mind flicked to the idea of dating. Gross. If their divorce *did* go through, she would probably be forced to return to Birch Harbor. A tourist community. She could picture it now. Friday night JEOPARDY! and popcorn gave way to squeezing into too-tight jeans and a blouse that hid her budding love handles. Fifteen minutes of makeup application and another fifteen minutes of blowing out her hair and for what? To make small talk with a weekender who didn't know a rowboat from a kayak?

Megan gagged at the idea.

Sure, other people might enjoy fraternizing their weekends away. In fact, Megan would love to *watch* that. But she'd like to do so comfortably, from a secure marriage that promised evening snuggles and an early bedtime.

Her dreams of a matchmaking business, her memories of luxe vacations and room service, and her ritual of cuddling on the couch with the love of her life had left a hollow cavern in her chest. The things she once had but could never get back.

Currently, as she and Amelia and Clara began their walk up the street to The Bungalows, Megan tried to push away her own drama.

They left the house fully clothed (eating lunch in a tankini top and sarong was the norm for Village eateries but still felt awkward now that Megan was *older* and a little less *local*), Megan cleared her throat and directed a pointed question to Amelia.

"Have you heard from Michael yet?"

Amelia shook her head. "No. Well, yes. I mean we checked in briefly on the phone. He is having lunch with a client then hitting the research. His plan is to get in touch with the Liesel Hart woman, but I had some other ideas."

"What? You think she's irrelevant?" Clara asked.

"I don't know. Maybe. Maybe not. I figure we could approach a couple different angles in the meantime."

Megan could read Amelia's mind. "Uncle Hugh."

"Yep." Amelia grinned. "Do you have his email address? Phone number?"

The question was for Megan, but Clara chimed in. "I doubt he has email. He's pretty old. But a phone number probably. In Mom's address book. It's in the cottage. I'm sure of it."

"Perfect. We'll find his information and maybe some other Actons. If anyone knows Liesel Hart, it'll be one of them. I'm sure Mom's side wouldn't."

Amelia made a good point. Not only had most of the Hannigans moved far away from Birch Harbor, but clearly whoever was bequeathed the lighthouse wouldn't be connected to *them*. It had to be someone on their dad's side of the family.

"Is that it then?" Megan asked. They'd made their way to the fourplex where Clara could get changed. From there, they'd go to the cottage. Initially, Megan and Amelia figured they could look around for anything pertaining to the lighthouse.

Amelia and Megan plopped onto Clara's sofa once inside. "No. There's something else we can do."

Megan studied Amelia, who now wore a poker face. After several taunting beats, Megan finally gave her sister's shoulder a soft push. "Well, what *is* it?"

The older woman's smile slipped off her face, and her voice dropped an octave. "I want to get my hands on Dad's case files."

Her eyebrows crowded together as Megan narrowed a serious gaze on Amelia. "What are you *talking* about? *Case* files? This isn't CSI Birch Harbor." Amelia had lost it. Their dad was a deadbeat, at best. Their mom shunned him and manipulated him into running away and never looking back. Megan's gut told her once they got in touch with their long-lost paternal relatives, that would all become crystal clear. In fact, maybe good old Wendell Acton was alive and well and living like a hippy on Mackinac Island for all they knew, totally happy to be entirely separated from the nut job daughters that his nut job estranged wife had raised. *Without* him. "You're crazy," Megan added for good measure.

"Maybe I am. But I'm also sick of being an orphan." Amelia shook her hair off her shoulders and threw up a hand.

"And now you're being dramatic. *Sick of being an orphan*? Mom died less than a month ago."

"That's not what I mean," Amelia shook her head, her eyes squinting with sassy attitude.

"Then what *do* you mean? What are you *suggesting*, Amelia?"

Clara entered the room, and Megan glanced back at her. Suddenly, the energy had changed. The warm walk on the beach was a cold memory. The sweet iced tea and sounds from the harbor had washed away as they sat in Clara's tiny one-bedroom. A lighthearted, hope-filled investigation into the fate of their well-meaning dad was suddenly devolving into the stuff of one of Megan's favorite true-crime TV shows. If it wasn't her life, Megan would be all in.

But it *was* her life. It was *their* life.

Megan's phone buzzed in her hand. She glanced down at the screen. It had been a long time since his name was a welcome reprieve. And now, it felt like her only escape from Amelia's over-the-top plan.

She looked up to Amelia and then again back to Clara.

"I have to take this."

"Who is it?" Amelia's eyes grew wide, and Megan wanted to slap some sense into her. She was turning family history into a crime drama.

Megan hissed her reply. "It's my *husband*."

Chapter 28—Amelia

After Megan stormed out the back door and onto the patio to take her call, Amelia turned to Clara. "You're with me on this, right?"

Clara's eyes grew wide. "What is going on?"

"I'm going to ask Michael how we can get our hands on the police reports that Mom and Grandma and Grandpa Acton made when Dad died." She knew she sounded like Velma from *Scooby Doo*, but Amelia was okay with that. She had every right to use her time in Birch Harbor to get some long-awaited answers. If her sisters weren't on board, that was their problem, but it did surprise Amelia that Megan, who often thrived within her own ghoulish canvas of black outfits and dark nail polish, was so against a renewed investigation.

Clara, however, seemed stunned as well. "There were police reports?" Her smooth face grew worry lines, and she crossed her arms protectively over her chest.

Amelia tried to explain as gently as possible. "Well, yes, Clara. When we were in Arizona—just days after Kate went into labor with you—that's when Mom got the call from the Actons that Dad went missing."

"What did they say? What happened exactly?"

"We don't know. That's the thing. Back then, Mom wanted to protect us from it. But we were old enough to know some things, and the police ended up questioning each of us, anyway."

"Questioning you? Like... *detectives* questioned you, or...?" Clara's cheeks grew rosy, and Amelia realized just how young and sheltered her littlest sister—her biological *niece*, technically—really was. It was odd to begin looking at Clara like she wasn't the baby of the four girls. It was odd to start reframing her back into the position of Kate's *child*. Yet, the recent revelations gave her no choice but to grapple with the truth. Perhaps that's what spurred her on in her mission to dig around. Then again maybe it was the suggestive diary entry Nora had left behind. Or the watch they happened to uncover. Or Clara's insistence that Wendell Acton's wedding band was nowhere to be seen just like the gun left to Amelia in the will.

Oh yes, she'd already dug around for the gun. Late the night before, she spent over an hour searching box after box in the basement, coming up empty handed. If all three of their father's earmarked effects could be accounted for... then she'd have something to go on.

But so far, all she had was a hunch and a waterlogged timepiece. Maybe she *was* crazy.

"All I'm saying is, let's check the cottage for the wedding band and his gun. Let's call some relatives. And, if it's even possible, let's have Michael pull up the records. We have a right to know what they learned about Dad. Just because Mom didn't tell us doesn't mean we don't deserve to *know*, Clara."

The pleading was useless, and Amelia could see that. Anyway, Wendell Acton wasn't even Clara's dad at all. She had little stake in the matter.

An innocent grin lifted Clara's face from its bewilderment. "You know? The last few days have been rough. The last few weeks. Months. *Years*. Amelia, all my life I never knew my dad. Then I was thrown a curveball, and it turns out I *can* know him—Matt, I'm talking about. None of us ever had that opportunity, so I get it. I am not into scary stuff like Megan, but I *get* it. I'll help. I'll do whatever you need me to do."

"So will I." The voice came from the back door. Megan, her expression steely.

Amelia stood from the couch. "You will?" She looked from Clara to Megan and back again. "Both of you?"

Clara glanced over her shoulder at Megan. "I take it the call didn't go like you'd hoped?" Amelia understood Clara to mean that Brian and Megan had argued and that Megan was choosing her sisters over her soon-to-be-ex.

"No," Megan answered. "It didn't go like I'd hoped."

Amelia offered a pained expression in solidarity, but Megan smiled. "Brian said he would help."

***

It turned out that Brian and Sarah were heading into town a little earlier than they'd planned. Megan had relayed to Amelia and Clara that Brian's conference was canceled. He and Sarah could stay the night in Birch Harbor. He'd spend the night in town and help with research the next day.

"Where will he *stay*?" Amelia asked, her eyes widening at the scandal.

"He can share my room at the house on the harbor."

Amelia grinned to herself.

"If it's all right, Sarah can stay with you at The Bungalows," Megan said to Clara. "That'll give us more space, anyway."

Amelia grew impatient with the sleeping arrangements conversation. "If Brian can help and Michael can help, then I think we can get to the bottom of this."

"One question," Megan asked as they headed out of the apartment and to Clara's car for the short drive up to Birch Creek.

"Yeah?" Amelia answered as she shot a quick text to Kate reminding her to let Dobi out for a potty break.

"What is it we're hoping to find?"

***

The cottage on Birch Creek huddled against the shadows of a creaking willow tree. It was as picturesque now as it had been when the family first bought the land, back when it was a hidden grove on a babbling creek. As a teenager, Amelia sometimes wondered if jigsaw puzzle art was based on similar locales. She still did.

Ivy crept up the sides of the house, and the navy-blue front door stood in stark contrast to the white wooden siding. Green potted ferns, shaggier than Amelia remembered from her most recent visit, waited like toy soldiers on either side of the welcome mat.

Clara let them in slowly, flipping on a tiffany lamp near the door and tossing her keys onto a side table as if she was home.

Technically, Amelia realized, Clara *was* home. She didn't begrudge her sister a perfect nest like the cottage. It was so *Clara*, after all. But some degree of sadness tugged at Amelia's heart. She didn't have a home. Not yet. She didn't have a quaint little cottage that was all her own. Perfectly eccentric and oddball and *Amelia*.

Who was she kidding? She also didn't have a job. Or the prospect of a job. All Amelia had was a task: decode Nora's final note to the sisters. The lighthouse on the lake. They had a claim to it, apparently. Nora insisted as much, though her mind was probably addled and her memory weak and discordant.

Once inside, Megan said she'd take the guest bedroom. Clara would take the living room and kitchen, where it was her job to unearth the address book so they could call their great uncle and others. Amelia wanted to dig into the master bedroom. Clara's own temporary room there, where she'd slept some nights during her caretaking spell for their mother, was no priority in terms of their search. What the three needed to focus on were boxes, dressers, bins, and anything else where Nora could have hidden things.

Amelia got to work immediately, carefully combing through drawers of shirts and pants, undergarments, and socks. Most of them were clearly Nora's. Some were men's items, but Amelia didn't recognize anything as specifically belonging to their father. Not yet.

Shoeboxes of photographs lined the floor of the closet, but Amelia knew better than to get sucked into that time warp of a chore. Her focus was on three things: a man's wedding band, Nora's missing letters, and the gun. The gun felt least relevant, but at least if they found it, they knew that Nora's will wasn't entirely off base.

"I've got it!" Clara's voice rang out from down the hall. Amelia tossed a stack of hangers onto the bed and rushed to the kitchen.

"What?" She and Megan met there together. Clara was pressing a hardcover notebook to the table.

"Her address book."

"Here, let me." Amelia took over, thumbing directly to the first tab. "A. Actons. I'm starting with Hugh."

"Are we sure he's still alive?" Megan asked. The question was no joke. Despite being the baby of the family, Hugh was still their father's uncle and elderly at minimum, potentially infirm. The sisters had no way of knowing, since they spent little time reminiscing with the Acton relatives who did show up for the funeral.

Things were *that* tense.

Shrugging, Amelia answered, "If he died, I'm sure we would have heard."

She returned her attention to the address book. *Hugh and Clarice Acton.* Amelia slipped her phone from her pocket and started pressing her uncle's phone number into her keypad.

The other two waited worriedly.

One ring. Two rings.

"Hello?" The slow, sweet, crackling voice of an old woman came on the phone.

"Aunt Clarice?" Amelia's voice came out high and tight.

A pause on the other end.

Amelia swallowed. "Is this Clarice Acton?"

"Yes?"

"Aunt Clarice, this is Amelia, um. Amelia Hannigan. Wendell's daughter?" She pressed her palm to her forehead, ignoring her sisters' bewildered expressions.

"Amelia?"

"Yes. Nora and Wendell Acton's daughter. Hi. I know this is a little... awkward, but I'm trying to get in touch with Uncle Hugh. Is he home? It's important."

"Oh," Clarice's voice rose an octave. Amelia braced for an extended greeting. But the woman cut to the chase. "Yes, yes Hugh is home." She chuckled quietly, as though it was silly for Amelia to even suggest he'd be out and about. "Just a moment while I get him for you, darling."

Amelia let out a sigh and flashed a thumbs up to her sisters.

A minute later, a garbled, heavy voice came on the line. "This is Hugh."

Amelia's heart sank. He sounded old and weak, and guilt swelled in her heart. They really should have been in touch more often. There was no excuse.

"Uncle Hugh, this is Amelia. Wendell's daughter?"

A pause.

"Amelia?" A wheezing cough cut him off briefly, but he recovered. "Amelia, of course. How *are* you holding up?"

Hugh and Clarice had not attended Nora's funeral, but they were surely aware, and his kind implication now acted as proof.

"Well, I'm okay." She pushed ahead before tears started to climb up her throat. "Uncle Hugh, I'm calling about the lighthouse. The lighthouse on the lake, here in Birch Harbor?"

"Hm?" he grunted through a fresh round of phlegm. The old man coughed a few times, and Amelia waited. "'Scuse me." He cleared his throat. "The lighthouse?"

"Yes. Where the Actons lived. Grandpa Acton, um—your brother? He ran the lighthouse just north of town. It's where our dad grew up."

"It's where he was last seen, too."

Amelia involuntarily recoiled. After a brief moment of pulling the phone away and checking her connection, she replied, "Last seen?" Could it be? Could great ol' Uncle Hugh have remembered the investigation?

"That's right." It sounded like he was taking a long pull of a drink. Just as she was about to prompt him, he spoke again, his voice clearer. "After his wife, I mean to say Nora. After Nora and you girls left town, he took up with my brother. My brother told us that young Wendell got real lonesome and couldn't stand to miss you girls."

Delicately, Amelia tapped the speaker button. Her sisters crowded around. Though he was delivering no new information, it felt intimate to hear the old man recount what they had been told, too. Amelia repeated what he said, framing it as a question for Megan and Clara's benefit.

"Yes, you've got it right," Hugh replied. "I don't think he stayed at the lighthouse round the clock or anything. But he spent most of his time there. He was fixing his boat, last they seen of him."

Megan's hand flew to her mouth, and Clara's jaw dropped. Fixing his boat? That *was* new information. Amelia felt her breaths grow shallow, like there was some secret that had been hidden from her. By the whole world. She, and her sisters, had been too shielded. Too protected. They were made to believe he left. But Hugh's words sliced through her chest like a knife. *Lonesome. Last seen.*

She stuck her hand in her pocket and retrieved the watch, holding it in the palm of her hand for her sisters to see. Nodding at them and forcing herself to swallow, she continued the conversation with Uncle Hugh. "So, Uncle Hugh, what did everyone make of the whole thing? I mean... you didn't *hear* from him again? My dad? Wendell, I mean?"

His reply came instantly. "Well of course not. My brother and his wife called the police and everything. Your mom was worried as all get out," he added.

"What happened after that?"

"Nothing happened," the old man replied. "They kept looking for him, and they never found him. We looked, too. All of us. We came down and did the search party thing, but the fact was it seemed he'd run off."

Amelia exchanged a knowing look with Megan. That was the same story they were handed.

Could it be? Could their otherwise loving, affectionate, supportive father be a deadbeat dad?

She knew there was little more Uncle Hugh could offer, but still she tried. "Uncle Hugh, was there any, um... *evidence* that proved he ran away?"

A wheezing cough came in reply, and he choked it out for a moment before clearing his throat. "Well, there was no evidence he *stayed.*" A dry chuckle followed, but the sisters did not laugh.

Amelia considered that. She dug through her memory, and there she found the detail of his wallet being gone. Their grandparents claimed he'd kept a duffle bag at the lighthouse, and it was gone, too. But Wendell Acton was a smart man, and it made no sense that he wouldn't take his handgun, the only gun he owned. The wedding band was another matter. Perhaps, if he had left, he'd meant it as a message to Nora, an attack on her heart. Would he do that to his *daughters,* though?

"Thanks for your time today, Uncle Hugh." Amelia let out a sigh.

"You're welcome. It's no problem. And don't be a stranger. Call anytime you'd like, young lady." At that she smiled, but Megan was snapping her fingers and mouthing something.

Frowning, she stalled him. "Oh, Uncle Hugh, there's one more question we have." A name took shape on Megan's silent mouth, and Amelia nodded vigorously. "Have you ever heard of a woman named Liesel Hart?"

"No, I'm sorry."

Her shoulders collapsed forward, but she gave it one more try. "She holds the deed to the lighthouse now. Would you know anything about *that*? Did Grandma and Grandpa Acton sell it to her?

He paused before answering. "That would make no sense. If I recall, my brother was dead set on you girls getting the lighthouse if it were possible. But he didn't know, seeing as it belonged to the town or what-not."

"Did anyone else in the family have a claim to it?" Amelia asked. Why, if the Hannigan sisters didn't get it, would a *different* family member not get it? Unless Liesel Hart had some sort of in with the Coast Guard.

"If they had, no one would have wanted it. I sure didn't. Keeping up a lighthouse is hard work, you see. We did it all our lives. Rand was the only one of us what had any interest at all."

After she hung up, Amelia and the other two stared at the phone for a while.

"If he doesn't know Liesel, then I can't see what she has to do with all this. Mom must have been confused again." Megan settled on aimlessly tugging open kitchen drawers, searching with less fervor than they'd had when they arrived.

"Her diary entries weren't confused, though. Everything basically rang true," Amelia reasoned.

Clara copied Megan and pulled open a corner drawer that didn't slide easily. "Amelia, do you think we need this Liesel person in order to find out where Wendell went?" Clara kept jerking the drawer, but it didn't open. Amelia joined her there and slipped a hand inside, blindly shuffling around junk and successfully unsticking it. The drawer opened, and Amelia let Clara continue to rummage inside.

"I don't know anymore. If Uncle Hugh believes Dad just left, then maybe he did." Exhaustion set in. She was tired of running down dead-end leads. It was growing later by the minute, and she began to think it was a mistake to come back to Birch Harbor. Her mother's tantalizing note was nothing but a red herring for an heirloom that went to some stranger.

"I'm going to call Michael and let him know that he can stop re-searching. I don't want the lighthouse. Do either of you?"

Clara and Megan also seemed deflated. Maybe they never were as invested in the property as Amelia. Maybe she ought to book the next flight to New York and beg for her job back. She could get back on a diet and start auditioning again. It was what she knew, after all.

"Hey, look," Clara whipped around with a folded page. "A brochure for the old museum."

Amelia glanced at it. "That's neat." Then she grabbed her phone from the counter and began to walk outside, where she could talk to Michael in private.

"Wait, *look*," Clara said again, the brochure held close to her face. Megan joined and read over her shoulder.

"What is it?" Amelia asked, halfway to the front door.

"Mom was a donor. I had no idea."

"Neat. Keep looking in there. Maybe you'll find another diary entry that spells everything out for us. Maybe this little postmortem mind game can finally end," she snarled. Her bad mood had sprung out of the call with Hugh, but she forced herself to offer a quick apology to her sisters before shaking out her hands and tapping Michael's name on her phone.

"Hey, I just finished my last meeting." His warm voice melted the last of her irritation.

"I hope it went well. Listen, Michael. We've been digging around here at my mom's cottage up on Birch Creek. We haven't found anything useful yet, but we called our Uncle Hugh; he was our father's uncle, actually."

"Oh?" Background noise dulled Michael's tone, and Amelia wondered if he, too, was growing bored with the wild goose chase.

"He has never heard of Liesel Hart."

"Ah," he replied. "So, you think the trail has gone cold?"

"I think," Amelia started to answer, but a shriek cut her short. "Hold on a second, Michael."

She opened the door to another shriek, belonging to Clara. "I found another one! Amelia!"

Her phone pressed to her chest, Amelia dashed inside to determine the source of her sisters' commotion.

Chapter 29—Megan

"Look." Megan and Clara stood together just where Amelia had left them, at the corner of the kitchen counter where she had unjammed the junk drawer.

Megan's eyes dashed across the page before Clara began to read it aloud for them.

There was no date on the entry. Not even a month this time. Though riddled with ambiguities, it highlighted one crushing specific.

Nora's darkest fear.

Megan sank back as Clara started reading. The words came to life as she watched her sisters' reactions.

"'Overnight my life has fallen into shambles. First handling a lovesick, hormonal teenager and her two sisters in a different state. Managing the hospital bills and complications I've thrust upon us because of my own fears, and for what? To save a little face? I never should have left. I should have listened to Wendell. Is it too late? I hope not.'" Clara glanced up at them, and Megan winced.

"Keep going," Amelia urged, nibbling her thumbnail as she continued to hold the phone against her chest.

Clara lifted the paper back to her face. "'It's been a long time now, and things are settled well enough. Kate will be leaving for college. As far as the girls know, Wendell left us. But I *know* it's not true. And what is worse is that I received a crippling phone call today. I'm not one to say *no* to new adventures, or old ones for that matter, but I had to say *no* to this. I don't know what repercussions it will carry. Wendell's parents have written me off completely. I have half a mind to believe they think I killed poor Wendell. Killed him! Why else would the police interview us over and over and over again? I finally wised up and hired Mr. Matuszewski.'" At that, Clara froze.

Megan whipped her head to Amelia, her eyebrows falling in together. "Matuszewski? Like... *Michael*?"

Amelia shook her head, bewilderment filled her face, and she tapped her phone screen. "Michael, are you there?"

His voice came over the speaker. "I'm here. Is everything okay?"

"We just found another of Mom's journal entries, and it says that our mother hired someone during the investigation into our dad's disappearance. A lawyer, I mean."

He didn't reply right away, so Megan nodded at Amelia to continue.

"Michael, she wrote that she hired *Mr. Matuszewski*. That's not..."

"My grandfather," Michael replied. The words came out on a gasp. "Oh my—I can't believe she never told me."

Megan frowned at Amelia. "What does he mean? Wouldn't his *grandfather* have mentioned it?"

"Is that Megan?" Michael asked blindly.

Amelia held the phone closer to her mouth. "Yes. You're on speaker. Did you not know about this?" The three sisters shared a skeptical look.

"No, I didn't. But I wasn't close to my grandfather. Neither was my dad. But I suppose I should have known, anyway. I mean, wasn't it big news around here?"

He sounded genuinely confused. Megan had to give him that. She leaned closer to Amelia. "Who are you talking about when you said you couldn't believe *she* never told you?"

"Nora. Your mom."

Megan rolled her eyes, though not at Michael. Of course Nora wouldn't have told him. The whole thing was very hush hush. As far as the Hannigan women knew, their mother paid off the whole town to sink Wendell's disappearance into oblivion and sufficiently hide it from local memory.

"Don't be surprised about that," Amelia assured him. "Mom was never one to air her own dirty laundry. Others' maybe, but not hers."

He sighed across the line. "Well, she did a good job keeping it under wraps. For being relatively new to town, I consider myself in the loop."

"Don't beat yourself up. It's old news. And anyway," Megan added, "as far as anyone believes, it was not a scandal. It was a man who left his family. Those types of stories are a dime a dozen, right?"

As she said it, Megan thought about Brian and why she chose him. Even as a young woman, she knew she didn't want a walk-away Joe. It was a big reason Megan said yes to Brian from the get-go. Sure, they hit it off. Sure, he was handsome, and she certainly fell in love. *Hard.* But in the end, Megan might have gone on a million other dates. She might have swooned over a brooding musician or taken up with one of Amelia's actor friends over the years, someone with charm, someone with rhythm who could dance and send endless goosebumps across her flesh, but no. She chose a man who had more fidelity than smooth moves. She chose a man who believed in commitment.

The irony did not escape her. Of course, it wasn't Brian who pressed for a separation.

It was Megan.

She bit her lower lip and said a quiet, private prayer. A big one, to be sure. And even though it was not a good moment, even though they were on the precipice of solving a decades-old family mystery, she pulled her own phone out and studied the last text message she'd received, rubbing her thumb across it with hope and fear. Her entire body lit up in goosebumps.

"Is that all she wrote?" Michael asked, startling Megan. She double-checked the time on her phone then slid it back into her pocket.

Amelia answered for the group. "No. There's more."

"Go ahead," Megan urged. "Read it."

Clearing her throat, Clara went on. "'He'—she's referencing your grandpa—" Clara added for Michael's benefit, "'kept me out of trouble, which was all I needed him to do. Besides, there just wasn't much to it.

The police had no evidence of foul play, but they surely had evidence that Wendell planned to go.'"

"Oh, wow," Amelia interrupted, her breath heavy.

"Sh," Megan snapped. "Keep reading." Even though she knew what was coming next, she was anxious for Amelia and Clara to know it, too. And even Michael.

"'His overnight duffle was missing. His boat was missing. And he'd left his truck at the house on the harbor, complete with the key in the visor. It was like a movie. A hellish movie. They all forced me to accept that he couldn't handle the pressure I'd put him under. I refused, though. I still refuse. On my life, Wendell didn't leave us. Not because of me or his own druthers, of that I'm certain. And yet, they refuse to continue the search. They—the police, Wendell's parents, and even my own lawyer—feel adamant that Wendell was (and I quote) *fed up*. With me. With *me*! And do you want to know why? I'll tell you why. Two words: Gene Carmichael.'"

Chapter 30—Amelia

Amelia gasped theatrically, nearly dropping her phone. "No freaking way."

Clara held the page out to her. There was no more to read. Nora hadn't even signed it. It was her most revealing and raw entry yet. Of course, the letters written directly to the girls were specific and useful, but this was all rage. All Nora.

She had loved their father. And she did not believe he just disappeared. So, if neither of those were true, then only a few—albeit extreme—explanations existed.

"Gene *killed* Dad?" Megan asked, her mouth agape and her black-tipped fingers pressed over it like a horrible gate.

"No, he didn't." It was Michael. Amelia nearly forgot he was still on the phone.

"What do you mean?" she asked him. "How do you know?"

It was his turn to sigh. "I know Gene. Personally. He still lived in town when I first moved here. I rented his house for a few years once he left. Gene didn't kill anyone."

"Is that *all* you know?" Amelia asked pointedly, staring at the phone for a dramatic response.

"Well, yeah. I know he's a good guy."

Clara set the page on the counter and shuffled back and forth, her expression strained. "I've heard about Gene. I don't *know* him, but I hear about him at school sometimes. He was a very popular principal."

"If I recall, Mom hated him," Megan offered. "Wasn't that right, Amelia?"

Amelia shook her head. "I don't know if she hated him, but she definitely avoided academic events. I mean, I suppose you could deduce a connection there, but... seems farfetched to me." Amelia wasn't the sort to be reasonable and rational, but something told her Michael was good at reading people. If he thought Gene Carmichael was a good guy, then she was compelled to believe him.

"Do you know anything else about him?" she asked the phone.

Michael cleared his throat over the line. "I mean, I know he met someone on a dating app." He chuckled but cleared it away with a small cough. "Sorry, it struck me as funny at the time because he was older. He, um, well, he wasn't having any success in that department, so he looked up people from out of town, found someone, and he left the harbor to be with her. He didn't leave for good, though. He comes to town regularly to meet up with friends. I'm not sure if he ever married that woman, but I think he brings his pals and dates on his houseboat. He's a little cocky acting, and I don't really know why, but he stays in touch with the community."

"We know," Amelia replied. Despite trusting Michael's opinion, she suddenly felt gross for having been so kind and accommodating towards him. Overeager, really. It was the curse of the extrovert—being too friendly to people who may or may not deserve such friendliness. Then again, maybe he *did* deserve it. Maybe he *was* a good guy.

"So, what was Mom's beef with Gene Carmichael?" Megan asked.

Amelia shrugged and frowned. "He's in town *right* now. Why don't we ask him?"

***

Despite Michael's claim that Gene was harmless, he insisted on meeting Amelia and her sisters before they started their search. Logically, they'd go to the house on the harbor or the Village. But there were complications. One, Megan wouldn't be able to join them. She was meeting Brian and Sarah soon, then they planned to go to dinner after the cemetery visit. Amelia asked if she could postpone—that their task was critical.

As they stood together outside the cottage, Megan shrugged. "My future is more important than our past. I'm sorry." Amelia and Clara agreed to drop her at the house on the harbor before they laid out their investigation plans.

"Let's tell Michael to meet us at the Village," Clara suggested. "It's a short walk for us once we drop Megan, and Kate can easily join."

"I'll call her," Amelia replied as they got ready to leave the cottage, thumbing through her phone until it rang. But their conversation veered off. Yes, Kate was astonished and interested in following the lead. No, she didn't know anything about Gene Carmichael other than he was their principal. Maybe she could meet them, but she *did* have plans for later that evening.

"How can she be so disinterested?" Clara asked, once Megan had climbed out from the car and bid them a good night.

"I know. It makes me feel like this whole thing is no big deal. Megan seems to care enough, but she's more consumed by Brian and Sarah."

"It makes sense," Clara reasoned. "I mean, things are weird with them right now. And if Sarah is going to stay here for a while, then she'd better iron everything out, right?"

Amelia sighed. "Yeah, I guess." There she was, back home in Birch Harbor, bumming a room in Kate's new house and business enterprise while Kate gallivanted around town with her old flame and Clara, fresh into summer, tagged along like a tourist. Megan had been by her side, also in the throes of a major life overhaul initially. But then, in a span of twenty-four hours it seemed, she was all of a sudden more consumed by the man she claimed to despise than her very own sisters and their crumbling family history.

Feeling more lost than ever, Amelia realized there was just one place she could stand to be. The lighthouse.

Perhaps its deed sat in the dusty filing cabinet of some indifferent stranger, but Liesel Hart wasn't Wendell Acton's daughter. Amelia was.

"I know where we can meet," she said to Clara, striding to her little sister's car and sliding into the passenger seat.

Once they pulled out from the gravel drive of the house which both sisters grew up in, Clara tugged her sunglasses from her forehead onto her nose and looked over. "All right. Where to?"

"Drive north."

Chapter 31—Megan

She had a fifteen-minute head start on Brian and Sarah. So, technically, she could have stayed with Amelia and Clara for a little while longer. After all, Megan was certainly curious about Gene Carmichael's connection to their father's disappearance. More than curious, in fact. To know that Wendell didn't leave them would not change anything, of course. Then again, it could change everything.

But whether her father meant to leave his daughters behind didn't matter as much to her as it had when she was a teenager. Megan had a new life now. A full one, truly. She had a daughter of her own to care for and support. She had more jobs to apply for. And, mainly, she had a love interest. A man she'd been texting whom she'd known forever.

A man she had committed to.

And so, with that in mind, she chose to be dropped off back at the house on the harbor and freshen up. Anyway, she needed her own vehicle.

It was after four when Megan walked in. She called out to Kate, who answered from the kitchen.

"Hi." Megan grabbed her bag from the ground and glanced briefly at her older sister. "You are... glowing?" It came out as a question, and Kate laughed.

"Glowing? Well, thank you. I haven't heard that in a while." She pressed her hands to her cheeks as if it were something she could feel on her skin. Megan smiled at her sister. Kate deserved this happiness. After so many years of living with their mother's decision, she deserved it. Megan knew, deep down inside, that Kate and Matt belonged together. They always had. And now, they had a chance at it. There was no reason to tease. No questions to ask. Standing before her was a woman in love all over again. A second-chance romance sort of love.

Nothing—*nothing*—like she felt about Brian. Was there something tugging inside of her? Sure. Was it a warm glow?

No.

"I just popped in to grab a couple things before I drive up to the cemetery," she declared to Kate. "We've changed plans a few times. We were going to go tomorrow, but Brian felt it was urgent, I guess."

Kate nodded, her face falling.

Megan crossed to her and pulled her big sister into her for a hug. "I know," she whispered. "It sucks."

Pushing away, she studied Kate's time-worn face. Crow's feet hid behind black frames, and shallow lines spread the width of her forehead. For being under fifty, Kate looked both good and older for her age. She was stylish and pretty, but a long life played out. Perhaps that's what happened when you stripped a child of her childhood. And Megan didn't consider the teenage pregnancy to be the culprit there. No. Kate's lost childhood at the hands of parents who were gritty and hard driving. Her forced breakup. Her forced adoption. Her abandonment. Even Megan's own childhood was colored by Kate's various heartbreaks and mandates. That's what became of middle children. They bore the shrapnel of their older siblings' trials. They were like children of divorced parents. Collateral damage. Of course, children recovered from that sort of thing. Maybe they grew extra wrinkles, but they recovered. They were fine.

Sometimes, they were even better off.

But none of the Hannigans were better off.

Maybe Sarah wouldn't be, either.

***

The Birch Harbor Cemetery stood opposite the secondary school. Gunmetal gravestones and mossy markers rolled up and down slight grassy hills. In some sections, the headstones shone above fresh flowers. In other, older sections, the footstones were not only unremarkable but also unreadable, the names having faded with time.

The Hannigans had their own sprawling plot in the far-left corner, along the back iron fence. An aged willow hung heavily above Megan's grandparents, her Aunt Margaret and Aunt Jody, and her Uncle Garold. Other Hannigans had their plots nearby, but Megan and her sisters were generally raised apart from the extended family. Most of them were much, much older and very long dead, anyway.

Of course, her mother's grave was there, too. Fresh dirt piled loosely atop of the burial site. The groundskeepers hadn't yet rolled on a new layer of sod. Is that how they did it? It occurred to Megan that she wasn't even sure. Did the deceased get grass seed or sod? It felt important right then, as she stood there, staring at the recently placed monument.

Kate asked that they expedite the settling of Nora's resting spot. She told the mortuary she'd pay extra, but she didn't have to. Turned out that Nora was good friends with the funeral director, who also owned and oversaw the cemetery.

It was a beautiful memorial. Simple but somehow exquisite.

Mary,
Mother of God
and Mother of mercy,
pray for us and for the faithful departed.
Nora Katherine Hannigan

The date followed, and that was it. No indication she was a daughter or sister or wife or mother. It's how Nora wanted to be remembered. For herself, not her ties to Earth.

Megan worked hard to accept the wish that Nora preferred to be alone in death. Or at least, on her final earthly hallmark. She swallowed and wiped an errant tear from her cheek. Just as she felt an urge to sob, footsteps on the grass distracted her.

"Mom," Sarah whispered from Brian's side. They were holding hands. Brian had always been an affectionate father, but Megan couldn't remember the last time Sarah wanted to so much as give him a hug. The sight sent a pang to her heart. Sarah was a crier, and Brian knew this. She was crying now, harder by the moment. He released her hand and pulled her into his side.

During the funeral, Sarah had her cousins, Ben and Will, to distract her from much of the grief. Now, stuck with just her parents, she had nothing else to do but think upon the matter.

Sarah hadn't known Nora as well as Nora would have liked. The guilt trips were unending on this matter, and Megan was only then beginning to realize that they would last long after Nora's last words about it. Megan did feel bad for being so distant. Their broken relationship with her mother would haunt her for years. Perhaps always. It might be unbearable. Megan knew there was no solution to this. No fixing the fact that she didn't visit each time Nora asked for a visit. She didn't invite Nora to visit each time the woman hinted that she had a free Saturday.

Perhaps, that was another thing crippling Megan's ability to solidify the divorce paperwork. Perhaps, the guilt was also pushing her that much closer to her sisters.

"You okay?" Brian and Sarah now stood with Megan at Nora's feet. In many ways, it was picture perfect. A scene from a movie. Megan had quickly changed into a light black tunic. Sarah, for once in her life, was dressed appropriately without hounding from her mother. Simple black skinny jeans and a dark navy blouse. Brian wore dark gray khakis and a black polo. It was a miniature, pared-down version of the funeral. More intimate. More *real*. Megan's eyes welled up.

Brian's did, too.

Then, a miracle happened.

No, Nora didn't rise up from the grave. Though in life, she often wondered aloud if her death might bring about the Second Coming. She was Catholic enough to repent for the blaspheme, but human enough to joke about it on a regular basis, especially with Megan who appreciated the grim humor.

It was a miracle of a different kind. A lesser, simpler, smaller kind.

Brian, standing beside Megan, his shoulders heaving up and down as he hugged Sarah tightly with one arm, reached down and took Megan's hand in his.

Then, he squeezed it.

Tearfully, Megan squeezed back.

Chapter 32—Amelia

By the time they reached the lighthouse, Amelia felt a bit silly. It was a dramatic locale, and there was no sense in meeting so far from the marina where they hoped to find Gene.

However, once Clara parked the car, and Amelia caught a glimpse of Michael standing in the sand near the water, the late summer sun throwing his shadow into lazy waves, she felt differently.

"Can you wait here?" she asked Clara, her hand on her little sister's arm.

"Sure. Take your time."

Amelia pushed out of the little car and ran her hands up her waist, smoothing her stomach into the waist of her jeans beneath her white tee. A light burst of wind tousled her hair into her face, but she just shook it out, leaving it to fly around as she strode toward Michael.

Pulling her father's watch from her jeans, Amelia considered its worth. The other items from her mom's will ran through her mind, too. They never found his gun. Or his wedding band. But they hadn't finished looking. Anyway, Amelia thought, what difference would the discovery of otherwise mundane objects really make? None, probably. Their search would continue unless Gene Carmichael could answer some very big, very old questions.

But then, maybe getting in touch with Gene wouldn't end their search either. Maybe, the whole hunt was one borne of boredom and nothing more.

Then again, why would a lucid Nora Hannigan write those three possessions into her will? Why would she add the lighthouse if she knew it wasn't theirs for the taking?

Was it a wild goose chase? A game? Or Nora's way to control their lives from the grave?

Or was their mother, for *once*, trying to help?

And then there was the matter of this man. This virtual stranger who, apparently had taken a liking to Nora and extended his kindness to her all-but-estranged daughters.

He was different from any man Amelia had ever taken an interest in. Serious and careful. Intentional and surefooted. Older, but only just. Handsome.

Yet Amelia was able to set that aside. She didn't quite see those qualities. What she saw was a Birch Harbor local who wanted to help her. And, for *once*, she was accepting it.

What help could Michael offer though? The lighthouse was off the table, for all intents and purposes. And the estate was settled. Nothing to bill. No legalese to wade through.

"Michael," she called out. The late afternoon felt different up at the lighthouse. It was quiet. The air was thinner, maybe. The sky took on a red effect that didn't happen at the Village with all its bright lights and boats. Normally, Amelia didn't like quiet. Silence, to Amelia, was lonesome and suffocating. Silence meant no attention. It meant she had to be alone with her thoughts. With who she was.

Who she wasn't.

He turned slowly from the water, his hands tucked neatly into khaki shorts. He'd probably changed since being at the office. This was not lawyer Michael.

This was after hours, beach Michael. Friendly family research assistant.

"Amelia." His reply came like a gentle echo. "How was your day?"

In another universe, they wouldn't be meeting with Clara waiting in the car. They wouldn't be soaring off on some sort of spy mission. They'd be... discussing funding for the Birch Players next show. Or drinking wine in Adirondack chairs after throwing together a small-town film festival. Amelia began to recognize a chemistry between them that buzzed a little differently than her usual flings.

Brief though their time together had been, Michael felt like a partner. An equal.

The banal question was a welcome relief. After all, was there really any rush? Clara had given her full permission to soak in the setting. The lighthouse did *not* belong to them. This may be their last time there. Particularly if Amelia did decide to leave again.

"It was…" she searched for the right word to capture exactly how her day had gone. Moments from her life in New York City flashed through her mind like a running Venn Diagram. In New York, her day consisted of sleeping in, waiting tables, and trudging around for auditions until it was time to hit the bars with the younger set. She was eternally tired. Eternally hopeless. Eternally, and ironically, unhappy. "Exciting."

"Exciting?" he asked, his mouth curling on one side into a lazy grin.

"Yes, actually." Amelia smiled broadly. It was the truth. For the first time in a long time, her weekend was full of life. Real life. Not the empty life of a forty-something who chased twenty-somethings around a soulless city in search of a ripped-off version of her dream job.

"So, no luck on Liesel Hart?" He gestured toward the lighthouse which glowed with the back-light of the sinking sun.

Amelia shook her head. "Unless you have your grandfather's old paperwork." She offered a smile, but he shrugged.

"We can get her address and send her a letter to ask about it. Or call the Coast Guard. I'm sure they have a record of how this place came to change hands."

"Why are you helping me?" Amelia's smile fell away, and she stepped up to the line of water in the sand, tapping at it with her knock-off Birkenstocks, making miniature splashes.

He cleared his throat then chuckled. "Honestly?"

She smiled, waiting.

"I think it's interesting. This old place teetering on the edge of town. Your eccentric mom—" his face reddened. "Sorry."

Amelia laughed. "That's okay. She was kooky."

His shoulders dropped a little. "Well, I loved that about her. She always had these tall tales. I didn't spend a lot of time with her, but the appointments she made—and her drop-ins—well, they were memorable. She was a character. And charitable, too."

At that, Amelia couldn't hold back an eye roll. "That came later in life. When she got bored, I think."

"She talked about you and your sisters a lot. Sharon felt like she knew you four."

Michael's secretary was enough of a busybody that she probably did think she knew the Hannigan sisters. And if that was true, maybe she could be of some help with the mystery. But Sharon wasn't a local. She was a transplant. And the mystery was a local one that needed local knowledge. Insider stuff.

"Don't you have other things to do?" Amelia asked, turning to him.

"Not really. I'm not one to go out a lot. I like history and reading. I like to see shows, too, but we don't have that here. Culture, I guess. That's my thing. So, when we read your mother's final note, I was *captivated*, you know? I don't think there's a better way to spend your time than by meeting new people and, well, helping them."

He was skirting around something, and Amelia had a suspicion about what it could be. But it wasn't the time or place to pursue her hunch. Instead, she just nodded her head, accepting his half-truths for the time being.

"So where to?" he asked, apparently pleased that she wasn't pushing the matter.

Amelia shook the nagging feeling that they had an opportunity they were squandering, threw a longing gaze to the lighthouse then turned back to him. "The marina. I'm pretty sure he's there tonight."

"Right, you mentioned that. Are you sure you want to... confront him, though?"

She considered the question seriously, thankful that in light of Kate's absence from the whole ordeal *someone* was stepping up and offering a responsible vantage point.

"I don't know. Frankly, I don't know," she admitted at last, peering across the sand up to where Clara was parked. Her face appeared in the driver's seat, placid and patient as ever.

Michael crossed his arms over his chest and rocked back on his heels. "What do you think you'll learn from him?"

"Maybe nothing. But what I *want* to learn is why my mother named him as the cause of my father's disappearance. And why the police *didn't*."

Chapter 33—Clara

After a while, Amelia returned to the car. Clara started the ignition but waited, looking over at her sister for a moment.

"You look different all of a sudden."

Amelia whipped her head toward Clara. "What?"

"You look different. You *seem* different. What did you two talk about out there?" Clara wasn't the sort to pry, but it was true. Amelia had gone through some sort of transformation in the span of fifteen minutes on the beach at the lighthouse with the family lawyer.

Amelia eased back into her seat and stared out the window, directly at the old, rickety property. Clara followed her gaze. She'd been to the lighthouse less than a handful of times. Mostly, she'd driven by it on her way out of town, actually. Though she knew it was once part of her family's collection of harbor properties, Clara felt no real attachment to the place. Her visits there had never been tied to the Actons, whom she never quite considered to be her grandparents even before she learned of her true beginnings.

The white paint was peeling off the siding, that much was obvious from their position inside the car, yards away. And the house seemed to sink away from the tower into the sand. Clara spoke up. "Whoever does own it must not live there. Right?"

Amelia gave her a hard look. "Yeah. I mean, obviously."

"It looks like she doesn't even care about it. This Liesel woman."

Nodding, Amelia looked back at the lighthouse.

Clara went on. "It doesn't make sense, then."

"What doesn't?" Amelia asked.

"If this person bought the lighthouse which would have been when the Actons died... what? In the early 2000s? Well, why would it be sitting here empty? I never remember anyone coming in and taking over. I feel like we'd have known."

A lightbulb seemed to flash in Amelia's mind. "Oh my gosh. You could be right." Then she shook her head. "Mom wouldn't have cared, though. She was so... *burned* by the Actons, it wouldn't have made her radar, you know?"

"Mom was a gossip. First and foremost. If someone bought and moved into that place, she'd have known about it."

"Maybe they just never moved in? Maybe it was on the down low," Amelia argued.

"Maybe. Then why would they buy it at all?" Clara frowned and put the car in reverse.

"Properties change hands all the time with no fanfare. I bet she didn't know." Amelia patted her thighs as if she'd settled it. But Clara was less convinced.

***

In time, they'd made their way back to the house on the harbor, the *Inn*. According to her texts, Kate had plans to meet Matt for drinks at The Bottle. Clara cringed at it, still uncomfortable with their reunion, the truth, and the new normal that was taking shape in her little town among her oldest sister and this complete stranger.

Still, Kate wanted to be deep in the loop on the whole Gene Carmichael situation, so she'd told them to call her immediately with any news or if they needed backup. After all, she would be sitting but a stone's throw from the dock.

They hadn't heard from Megan yet, but she, too, had dinner plans at the Village. Clara was excited to see her niece—or cousin, as the case may be. But she knew her place was there with Amelia, as emotional support during a very bizarre turn of events. Anyway, Megan also declared she'd be nearby.

By the time they got out of her car, Michael had parked his truck on the street and Amelia had arranged for a family breakfast at seven o'clock sharp the next morning to debrief after that evening's events.

Clara felt that seven was way too early, and that a late-night gathering might be more appropriate. Anyway, what if they learned something that changed everything? Neither Amelia nor Clara could sleep on a juicy revelation.

Evening was falling slowly on the shore, the sun still hanging steadily above the horizon behind them as they walked to the marina, Clara in front, Amelia and Michael beside each other behind her. Clara didn't like the role of chaperone, which is what she was fast becoming, but once they arrived at the marina, Michael took her position and had Clara step back.

"If it's all right with both of you, maybe we should make a game plan, first?" he suggested.

Clara peered around him toward the marina office, looking casually to see if Jake Hennings was in there. Surely, he wasn't. Surely, he didn't work all day and all evening. Her heart sank, and she returned her attention to Michael. "A game plan is a great idea. How exactly are we going to spin this? Maybe we should just take his number and tell him we'd like to call him in the future."

"What?" Amelia asked. "That would be way weirder."

"I could easily contact him on your behalf," Michael offered. "I have his number and email address somewhere. I'm sure of it."

Amelia shook her head. "I believe in fate. And we bumped into him earlier today? What are the odds of seeing him, stopping and talking to him, then coming across Mom's journal entry?"

"Probably relatively high," Clara reasoned. "I mean, he comes to town all the time, and we were actively looking for some things in the cottage..."

Amelia shot Clara a look, and she knew well enough to shut up.

"It's your call, Amelia. You're the one who read Nora's letter about the lighthouse. You're the one who took this on. We're here for you, right Clara?" He flicked a glance to Clara who felt a sudden urge to prod Amelia on. A sudden sense of adventure. With Michael there, she felt safe. She imagined Amelia did, too.

"We're going in. I have to know. We all have to know. Even Kate and Megan who are off doing their own thing. This is our *Dad* we're talking about." The plea was meant for Clara, but when they locked expressions, awkwardness filled the space between the sisters. Wendell, in fact, was *not* Clara's father. But even so, Amelia *was* Clara's sister. And finding him mattered. It was her fate. *Their* fate, perhaps. And if this Gene Carmichael character had the answer, then they had to pursue him.

"I'm in. Let's do it."

Chapter 34—Amelia

The plan was simple. They'd walk to Gene Carmichael's houseboat and call out to him. Michael would re-introduce himself then hand it over to Amelia. If there was one thing she could pull off, it was improv. It was her best talent. And here was her one shot to use it. An important shot, too.

Amelia felt her skin tingle with life as the trio strode past the marina office and onto the broad wooden pier. For a small town, Birch Harbor offered several docks with dozens of boat slips, each organized neatly by an assigned letter.

The platform carried them off land and into the life of Great People, as Wendell had always called boaters and sailors of Lake Huron, including himself. It was a lame joke back when Amelia was a girl. But as she grew up, she came to understand it. She'd seen her fair share of lake people across the States. They were nice, hard-working, salt-of-the-earth types.

Still, her dad had been right. *We aren't lake people. Lake people crack open a Coors Light on their stern, toss a line in the water, and buzz around in circles spitting cud starboard until they have to pack it in for the day. Those of us who sail the Great Lakes aren't lake people. We're Great People!* Amelia smiled at the silly memory, happy to greet it. Funny enough, Wendell was no snob. He just took life on the lake seriously. The water was not just for recreation to Wendell. It was life.

As they walked, Lake Huron slipped in and around the docks, lapping up against the moorings in the hollow spaces between the boats, its rhythm churning a nautical time.

Turning onto C Dock, Amelia lifted a finger. "Here it is. Right, Clara? This was the one?" The third dock on the right hosted larger vessels in ample berths, but Gene Carmichael's was the only houseboat currently moored. Modest as far as houseboats went, Amelia began to worry if it was even his.

Clara nodded urgently. "Yes, look." She pointed, too, to the side of the boat where the name glowed from beneath a string of lights. "*Harbor Hawk.*"

Amelia nodded at the name, faintly remembering it from earlier in the day.

The boat was alive with lights and the faint sound of jazz, even though the sun had yet to set. Muffled voices roared up and lowered like a tide. She was silently grateful they were back. It was luck. Or, fate. *Meant to be.* Amelia clung to her belief in destiny and that everything was working out because it was meant to.

"Want me to do it?" Michael asked, standing impossibly close to Amelia.

Emotion overcame her, and she squeezed his hand. "Thanks, but I've got it." Then, stepping up to the edge of the dock, she shook her arms out and cleared her throat. A quick glance back to Clara, who gave her a thumbs up, nearly pushed Amelia to laugh at herself for what she was about to say. "Um," she began, biting her lip and then again shaking out her arms. "Okay, here we go. *AHOY!*"

Behind her, Clara and Michael fell into veritable hysterics. Amelia turned and glared. "It's all I could think of!" She shushed them and tried again, pulling volume from her diaphragm and bellowing deeply over the ambient sounds. "Ahoy! Mr. Carmichael!"

Like magic, her old principal, the man named in her mother's angry, missing diary entry appeared from a low door amidships. His face glowed, the sun behind him creating a halo and changing his entire look. Gone was the wan, older gentleman who kindly ruled over her high school and fumbled through recalling who she was earlier that day. In just hours he'd turned into a flamboyant houseboat partier, not yet past his prime. In that moment, Amelia saw an unwelcome connection between Mr. Carmichael the principal and her mother the country club queen. She frowned.

"Hi!" he called back, moving through his boat and to the side carefully, shedding some of the charisma he'd boasted just moments before as he took care to avoid falling. "Amelia, right?"

Impressed he'd remembered her name this time, she nodded and glanced behind her.

Michael took a step forward. "Gene. How are you?"

Mr. Carmichael cocked his head to the side, studying Michael for a moment then snapping his fingers. "Well I'll be darned. Matuszewski's boy. Michael, hello." He passed a gnarled hand over the side of the boat and onto the dock, and Michael shook it. "I'm here with Amelia and her sister," he cleared his throat, "Clara. As a friend, mainly. We, or they, rather, had a question."

Skepticism took the place of Mr. Carmichael's smiles, and it was Amelia's cue to launch into her scene.

"Mr. Carmichael, I'm sure this isn't a good time, but we're following up on some loose threads regarding my mother's estate. And, I suppose, my father's, too." She paused a beat, studying him.

His face fell. "I'm so sorry to hear about Nora. You know, I intended to come to the funeral, but..."

She cut him off, uninterested in his excuse. "Oh, it's fine. We were going through some of my mother's personal effects in an effort to pin down how the old lighthouse up north came to be sold. We've found a name—a woman called Liesel Hart—but it turned into a dead end. In some of her..." Amelia glanced briefly to Clara, finding the right word, "*paperwork*," she swallowed, "she named you as, um, well." Amelia hadn't lost him yet. In fact, Gene Carmichael had narrowed his gaze on her and gripped onto a piling to steady himself. He waited the brief moment it took her to find exactly what she was going to say. "Mr. Carmichael, our mother told us to find you and ask you."

He smirked at Michael, who replied by crossing his arms and setting his jaw.

"Ask me what?" Gene replied.

"Mr. Carmichael, what happened to our father, Wendell Acton?"

***

Some minutes later, Amelia, Michael, and Clara were seated at the bow, each with a margarita in hand.

Gene Carmichael had shocked Amelia when instead of begging off of the question, he invited them to sit and talk.

She accepted. Their host busied himself indicating to his guests that he had a pressing matter to attend to, then he brought out a round of drinks. Amelia caught Clara pucker, but all three of them acted politely and sipped periodically from their sour beverages while Gene Carmichael began.

"I'm not sure what you know and what you don't," he began, waiting for an answer from Amelia. She swallowed and exchanged a nervous glance with Clara. Maybe this was bigger than an impromptu houseboat meeting. Maybe Kate and Megan should be there.

Sucking in a deep breath, Amelia pulled from some inner reserve of leadership and maturity that she'd often hidden from her daily interactions. "If you know something, Mr. Carmichael, and it's important, then I think I need my other sisters to hear it."

Michael, who sat beside her, covered Amelia's hand in his own. Her heart pounded against her chest wall, and she flicked a glance to Clara, who nodded her on.

"Well, like I said, I'm not sure if what I know is important. Or *news* or whatnot. You're welcome to invite your sisters here. My company can entertain themselves. We dock at Birch Harbor no less than twice a week, you know. Usually more often than that.

"Where do you live?" Amelia asked.

"Heirloom Island."

Her mouth fell open. "I didn't know you were so close. I figured you'd left for a bigger city or something."

"My heart belongs to Birch Harbor. But I couldn't stand to be here day in, day out. Not once I retired."

Amelia nodded as if she understood, but she did not. She turned to Clara. "I think," she began, worried she was about to make the wrong decision. In her life, Amelia, social though she was, had usually acted independently. It rarely served her well, if her long history of loser exboyfriends and dead-end waitressing jobs and lack of acting gigs was any indication. But Amelia liked it that way. She liked to fight her way to a happy ending. And though for many years, her path hadn't ended in a pot of gold, there she was. Back in Birch Harbor, with her sisters and a new friend in Michael-the-lawyer. She still didn't have a home. She still didn't have a job.

But there she was, on the verge of having the truth.

"We can't do this without them," she continued, holding Clara's nervous stare, "why don't you call Megan and Kate. Michael and I will wait here with Gene. Tell them it's important."

Clara nodded and stood, pacing a short distance away and leaving Amelia and Michael to sit with Gene, who seemed nice enough, but who also seemed to bear a deep, dark secret.

***

Soon enough, a commotion broke out on the jetty. Amelia heard her name and craned her neck to see Megan, clad in a black dress and Kate, in a white dress, appear in front of a small group of people. Squinting further, she recognized Matt Fiorillo, Brian, and Sarah huddling near the man she'd asked for help earlier. The marina manager. Jake.

"There they are." Amelia pointed and waved, and Clara, who was still standing, deboarded the boat and waved, too. Calling out to them.

Megan and Kate sped down the jetty toward Dock C and turned. "Is everything okay?" Kate demanded, her eyes flashing from even yards away.

"Over here!" Amelia cried, standing near Michael, her body tense and awash in goosebumps at that moment. Michael and Gene also stood, smiling tightly.

With Michael's help, Amelia's three sisters came aboard and joined them.

"Care for a cocktail?" Gene asked.

Kate and Megan sat, bewildered, each politely declining.

"What's going on?" Kate asked. Amelia noticed her fresh face of makeup and blown out hair. She'd been on a date. With Matt. Guilt briefly pooled in Amelia's stomach for tearing her sister away, but she could go back to him. She *would* go back to him. After Gene spilled the beans.

"Gene wants to tell us something," Amelia answered simply, lifting her palm and returning to her seat.

"I'm going to excuse myself, ladies. Gene." Michael nodded to each then dropped his voice. "Amelia, if you need anything, I'll be just over there." He gestured to the shore, where the others stood confused.

She thanked him and they waited until Michael had left.

"Mr. Carmichael? I think we're ready."

He smiled sadly, let out a long sigh and hitched his trousers before sitting across from the four of them.

And then he walked them down a very ambling, very twisted memory lane.

Chapter 35—Nora

I'll bury this entry. I'll bury it deep in my hope chest and lock it up. It can sit under something heavy, so it stays in place, and I'll tell Clara to be sure to find the hope chest. I'll tell her when she's older. When I'm older and on my deathbed. Maybe I'll go down in history as one of those enchanting women who call a loved one to her deathbed to share a shocking secret.

No, that's a little too "tabloid" for my style. But I'll tuck this page underneath something heavy, like Wendell's revolver or a paperweight, deep in the bottom of the hope chest. And there it will stay until they pull it out and see for themselves that I wasn't selfish.

I have to hide this, because if I don't and it's discovered, then everything could fall apart, and I can't have things fall apart. Not when they've finally started to calm down.

Yet, I want it down on paper so that the truth isn't lost forever. One day, my girls will want to know. They probably want to know now, but it wouldn't help them. What will help them is for us to push on and live our lives as normally as possible. How could I live with myself if I interrupt Kate and her newly perfect life? Or Amelia, bless her wild heart, who's following her dreams? And Megan, secure, dark Megan with her clever husband and babbling baby girl? I won't do it. And Clara's still in school. She deserves her normalcy. Needs it, really.

I know what it's like to hold a secret to my breast and have my entire life spin out of control, and I'll never put that on any of my children. But one day, I'll die, and they won't know about the lighthouse. They won't know about what happened to me and what I had to do. So here it is.

When I was a teenager, I thought I met a boy. I probably wrote about all this back then. He was a tourist, and he was cute. I fell pregnant, and I told my mother. This was a mistake, in retrospect. I thought she would help me and raise the baby with me. We could pass her off as my youngest sister. I thought everything would be okay.

My mother was enraged and shared the news with my father. They threatened us. They told the boy and me that we had two choices, get married and move out or give the baby away.

The boy wanted to marry me. Maybe I ought to have done that. But to marry him would be to move off the lake and somewhere else. He was going to school to become a teacher, and in the end, I didn't love him.

I told my parents that I would not marry him, but I would keep the child.

That didn't happen. It turned out that they made the decision for us, adopting the baby out to a good family from the south. A big, Catholic family happy to take in another Catholic baby.

For some years after, I searched for my daughter, never to find her. Instead, I found the man I would fall in love with, Wendell Acton.

I made another mistake, though. I never told Wendell about my past. I was too worried it would be a deal-breaker for him and that I'd be faced with new heartache. I feared I would drown from all the tragedy, and so I kept it a secret.

By the time Wendell and I were married, and we had our own three beautiful girls, I found a new comfort in my new life. I could move on. I had to move on from my first bouncing baby girl.

It was by then that that child would have turned eighteen, but the no-contact order had been two-way. My parents and her adoptive parents had agreed that neither we nor they would ever get in touch. To do so would break the law.

On her birth certificate, my parents and I agreed to leave the boy's name off in favor of a humiliating note: Father Unknown. I'll never forgive them for that, but then I'd never have wanted to include the boy's name. The simple truth was that I did not love him. Despite my preference for excitement and adventure, it was never a summer boy I wanted.

It was a local one. And once I found Wendell, all I wanted was for the past to be buried for good.

Then, Kate unwittingly followed in my footsteps. To me, there was just one option, to raise the baby as Kate's sister, as I had wanted. Wendell disagreed and thought perhaps Kate and Matthew ought to be together. But I thought then that we shouldn't force that on Kate. I sometimes wonder if I was wrong. If that's why Wendell left?

And unfortunately, I'll never know. As much as I wish I could answer that mystery in this note, I cannot. All I know is that wherever Wendell is now, he's not with me. And I can't stand it. So, I'll ask my daughters to look for him. In my own way, I'll see to it that they find their father and come to know that whatever happened, he surely loved them. As much as I do.

Kate, Amelia, Megan, and Clara: Go find him. Please.

Chapter 36—Amelia

"I met your mother one summer when I came here with my folks. We lived in the city, but my mom heard about a bed-and-breakfast somewhere in town. I don't think it's up and running any longer. I was a bored teenager, and I ran into this beautiful blonde local. Townie, I suppose. Anyway, I fell hard for her, but she treated me as little more than a plaything." He chuckled, but the sisters remained perfectly still. "Anyway," he went on, passing his hand along his jaw as a deep frown took hold, "your mother got pregnant."

Amelia's face fell slack, and she felt dizzy. It came on hard and suddenly, and she tried to focus her eyes. Clara, beside her, gasped audibly. Kate interrupted. "You're joking." Her voice was flat, her expression pained. Amelia reached out her hand to Kate, squeezing her arm.

Megan added, her voice a whisper. "That can't be."

"Yes. It's true. After we found out, I asked her to keep the baby. She said she would, but that she didn't want to be with me. She thought we couldn't make it work, especially since I didn't live here." He lifted a helpless hand and dropped it to his knee. "Honestly, after she told me, I didn't learn much more. She sent one letter, months later. In it, she said her parents were going to force her to give the child up. A day didn't go by that I didn't call her, write a letter, or mope about the whole thing. Once I finished with my degree, I applied to teach at Birch Harbor High. I—" he looked down at his hands. "I became a little obsessed over the whole thing."

Amelia tried to offer a smile, but he didn't look up.

"Your mother married Wendell, of course, and I had to find a way to move on. I dated, sure, but it took many years until I met my current wife. Long after I'd gone back for my principal's certificate and been promoted. Watching you three—" he pointed along to Kate, Amelia, and Megan with precision — "move up through the school nearly killed me. But I made it and retired and married and moved. Never quite moved on, though."

Amelia frowned. "So why would she write that you had something to do with Wendell's leaving?"

He shook his head. "Well, I'm not sure. I never contacted him or her. Ever. I swear it." The sisters kept quiet, waiting for a better answer. At last, he heaved a sigh. "I can share my theory, but it's pure speculation."

"Mr. Carmichael," Amelia pleaded. "We're desperate. Our lives changed in the matter of a summer. We went from a big, happy, hardworking, normal family to a broken one. Our mother took us to Arizona to hide Kate's pregnancy. She chose Kate's future *for* her, which now we can understand why... but everything changed. We came back, and we had a baby sister. We had to sneak away to a half-finished cottage inland. We had to lie to our friends and even to other family about why we were gone. But that was all fine and dandy compared to learning that our dad had left us. And then there were more lies, it felt like. We started thinking, Mr. Carmichael, that maybe he hadn't left. We started thinking—" Amelia glanced at her sisters, whose strained expressions mirrored her own inner plight, "—that maybe he *died*."

She let out a long, slow breath after her confession. Amelia knew it's what Kate and Megan and Clara believed, too. Deep down. Even if it wasn't something they discussed. No other reason rang true. And the police investigation came up empty. Even Wendell's own family came to accept that he just *left*. With his duffle, maybe even his gun and wedding band.

Waiting for Gene Carmichael to scoff and disagree, Amelia leaned back into her polyester seat. From where she was, she could see Michael and Matt and Brian and Sarah watching with focus. Though Amelia didn't regret coming to see Gene, she was ready for the ordeal to be over. Maybe they could go out for pizza after this and wash it all away, out to shore, with every other secret in their family history.

Gene held up his hands. "I've considered that, too," he replied. "I've wondered if maybe there were some unresolved feelings on Nora's end. Maybe he found out, but then, how would he? And if he did find out, why not confront Nora? Or me, for that matter?"

"Back up a moment," Kate interjected. "Are you saying you don't think Wendell ever knew about you or the baby?"

Amelia felt her chest swell in anxiety. Was that the key to this whole thing? She drew the watch from her pocket and held it out to Gene. "We found this at the lighthouse. Stuck under the dock. We can't find his wedding band or anything else that suggests something bad happened, but his brother says he was on his boat last they knew."

They were throwing a lot at him, but he could handle it. He looked first at Kate. "No. As far as I'm aware, Wendell never knew the truth."

"But we don't know for sure," she answered.

He shrugged. "And about his personal effects, that was the evidence the police used when they determined they weren't going to drag all of Lake Huron."

Amelia frowned. "They didn't drag the lake? Did they even look for him?"

Shaking his head, Gene replied, "*Everyone* looked for him. But neither your father nor his boat ever turned up. When they learned he'd taken his duffle, they called it a day and packed it in."

Amelia's face fell. "Okay, well," she tried to accept what he was saying, but it didn't feel like enough. She wracked her brain for any other question she could think of to nail down the facts. Kate beat her to the punch.

"What about the baby?" she asked him.

A moment paused before Gene answered. "I never heard from her. Nora never mentioned her. It was a closed adoption, and we weren't allowed to make any sort of contact. Period. I'm so sorry I can't help. realize this means you have another sister out there somewhere."

Clara let out a small sob. Amelia wrapped an arm around her, shushing her. They began to thank Gene, Kate apologizing for taking his time and asking if they might stay in touch in the future. He accepted, but while she took out her phone, a thought occurred to Amelia.

"Wait a minute," she hissed to herself.

Megan and Clara pulled themselves out of their deep disappointment and turned to look at her. "What is it?" Megan asked.

"I can't believe we didn't think of this. Kate," Amelia stood, grabbing Kate's wrist and keeping her from adding Gene Carmichael's number to her phone. "The baby. The baby girl."

"What are you saying?" Kate asked bewildered.

"I think we know who she is."

Chapter 37—Amelia

"Slice of Life, *now*." Amelia had all but run from the boat to the others waiting, directing everyone to the Village's pizzeria. It sat squarely in the middle of the plaza with ample outdoor seating. They didn't have to wait for a hostess, they could seat themselves and get straight down to business.

Which Amelia did.

Everyone had joined, except for the marina manager, who'd disappeared before Amelia rushed off the pier and into the plaza. Now, they were waiting for her to explain.

Kate held her hands out over the table. "Let's just calm down a minute. They don't even know what's going on," she lifted a hand to the motley group of men whose faces drew up in concern. Sarah, for her part, had plucked a menu from the hostess stand and was busying herself for an order. None of them had eaten dinner yet. Food felt like a priority even to Amelia. But it had to wait while she revealed her hunch.

Briefly, Amelia brought everyone up to speed, reviewing the truth about Nora and Gene's history and covering the fact that it seemed increasingly clear that Wendell might have died, by accident or, more darkly, otherwise.

"So, let me get this straight," Brian interjected. His tone was at once warm and also skeptical. Amelia glanced at Megan, who, impossibly, did *not* actually seem annoyed with him. "Your mom had a teen pregnancy with this Gene Carmichael guy and gave the child up for adoption, just like Kate—in a way, except she never got to see the baby again. Then, after you all returned from hiding Kate's pregnancy, your dad had vanished. Everyone thought he left you and your mom, but now you're saying some people think he actually died?"

Amelia began to nod, but it was Michael who offered an answer. He cleared his throat. "May I add something?"

"Please do," Amelia said, still sitting on her latest theory.

"When I came to town and resurrected my granddad's business, there was no hint of whatever happened with Wendell. When I eventually learned about it, through tidbits from Nora and now from Amelia, I felt like the answer was clear: he left. Now, I still think that's the truth. And if you can find the daughter Nora and Gene had, maybe you'll find out if she sprung the truth on Wendell. If so, then it makes even more sense for him to cut bait. I hate to even say that, but..."

Amelia sighed. "I see what you mean, Michael. But if what I'm thinking is true, then your idea makes less sense, actually."

"Amelia," Kate spat, "what in the *world* are you thinking?"

But before the sentence could even fly out of her mouth, Michael grabbed her hand. "Oh, my word. I know *exactly* what you're thinking."

They spoke at once, their words and inflection perfectly synchronized.

"Liesel Hart."

Chapter 38—Megan

The next twelve hours were a blur. The goal was to track down Liesel using any means necessary. They spent the evening doing some basic online searching, but all agreed to let it go for the night and take up the hunt first thing in the morning.

Anyway, a simple Google search returned nothing of value.

Sarah offered to apply her social media smarts for the effort, but they only got as far as finding a blurry tagged photo on Facebook at some church event. The sisters scoured her image but could deduce nothing more than a slender woman of around fifty years of age.

Michael had pulled up legal records where possible and discovered an address in a small town on the edge of the Ohio River: Hickory Grove, Indiana. They would set up putting together a letter and sending it, but all of them hoped to make contact sooner. As in, immediately.

That's where Brian came in.

The next morning, over a groggy breakfast of eggs and bacon (no one slept well, particularly Megan and Brian who were unused to sharing a tight space or sleeping in the same bed at all), Brian unpacked his laptop and booted it up, referencing a simple idea that wouldn't have taken a tech genius to figure out.

"All we need to know is who she works for," he announced.

"She has no LinkedIn profile," Sarah murmured into a steaming mug of coffee. Megan raised an eyebrow. Since when had her teenage daughter taken up the art of depending on caffeine?

Letting the matter go for the time being, Megan added, "Actually, Brian's onto something. We can find a business in the town where she lives and go from there. It's sort of exciting. I feel like a bounty hunter."

"That's perfect," Amelia answered. "Brian, can you pull up some local businesses?"

"Yeah, but what will you say? You can't lie, of course." Michael was there, too. He shifted his morning appointment to the afternoon. Even Matt Fiorillo showed up for breakfast. He'd waffled at first, since he didn't want to ditch his daughter. But Megan suggested he bring her along to meet Sarah. Clara loved the idea, too, and soon enough it was a big, sleepy brunch full of family and new friends. Everyone in the Hannigan sisters' circle was present and accounted for, anxious to help and, probably, anxious to solve the mystery.

Sarah and her new friend, Viviana, had taken to each other instantly, despite the age gap. They slipped out onto the back deck together, giggling as though they'd been friends all their lives. It was good for Sarah to take on the position of role model. She could use a chance to shine in that way after growing up as a single child and her mother's mini-me.

"I'm not going to lie," Amelia promised. "I won't have to. I'll say who I am and that I'm searching for my sister who was adopted at birth. I'll say I think she might be called Liesel Hart." Amelia smiled at Michael, and Megan caught an undertone of flirtation. She smiled for her sister, too.

"Sounds good, let's do it."

"Okay, here." Brian pointed to his computer screen. "Hickory Grove Antiques. It's the first business that comes up."

Amelia bit her lower lip and rocked back and forth in contemplation. "I feel like that's a pretty narrow result. Shouldn't we try something that's more of a mainstay for locals? Is there a grocery store? Or... gosh I don't know. I suppose no bank or post office is going to give out information."

"That's right. We'll have to be a little sneakier than that," Megan added.

Michael rolled his eyes and cleared his throat, and Megan giggled at his discomfort. Amelia shot her a look.

"It'll be fine. I'll call the antique shop, and we can go from there. All right? But I'm going to need a little breathing room here." Amelia shooed them off. Kate and Matt set about brewing a second pot of coffee. Clara pulled her phone out and wandered down the hall. And Megan and Brian opened the back door, stepping out and into the sunny morning together.

Sarah and her new friend were walking along the shore, and it drew Megan sharply back to her childhood. Her upbringing, fragmented in many ways, hadn't played out quite as a girl might hope. Had her daughter's? Was it too late?

As she stood with Brian on the edge of the deck at the Heirloom Inn, her sister's new business venture, as her other sister was just finding a project, Megan realized she had to find something for herself, too. And when Brian, her husband, the man she was so *ready* to divorce, picked up her hand and laced his fingers in hers, she knew that it was *not* too late. For anything.

Chapter 39—Amelia

Mere moments later, the phone was ringing against Amelia's ear. Her heart thrummed in her chest with the excitement of the first step in what could be a successful enterprise. If she performed well.

"Hickory Grove Antiques, this is Fern." The voice on the line was serious but warm.

"Hello. My name is Amelia Hannigan. I'm calling with a strange request," she began.

Fern laughed softly. "We tend to get those from time to time."

A smile softened Amelia's face. "All right, well here goes nothing."

Carefully, avoiding any salacious or oddly vague details, Amelia explained her situation just as she promised Michael, relaying the truth but in limited detail. When she was finished speaking, she sucked in a breath, bracing for a rejection.

Fate intervened.

"I know Liesel," Fern replied quietly.

Amelia's mouth opened and shut but no words came. She held a hand over the phone receiver and shouted for everyone to return quickly, and she tapped the speaker icon on the phone, finally finding her voice as her sisters and Michael and Matt crowded in around the table. "Oh my," Amelia answered, her breath shallow. Licking her lips, she shook her head and blinked. "You do?"

"Why, yes. Through church. We both serve on the Little Flock Ladies Auxiliary. We aren't close, per se... but I do know her."

Amelia felt her shoulders go slack; her entire body sagged.

Maybe it was *more* than fate that drew her back to Birch Harbor. That pushed her to say goodbye to New York and a studio apartment and move Dobi away from the city smog and late-night cigarette stench. Maybe it was never simply *meant to be*. Maybe it was a higher thing. Maybe someone was looking down, watching her, guiding her, and... *trusting* her, finally, to follow her gut instinct and make a good decision for once. Maybe this, all of it, was a good choice.

***

Her conversation with Fern was brief. The woman was kind and sympathetic and happy to help but not comfortable handing over Liesel's phone number to a veritable stranger. Amelia understood this and instead provided her number for Fern to relay to the elusive Liesel Hart.

Now, all they had to do was wait.

And wait.

And wait.

In the end, two whole weeks had passed since the morning Amelia had placed a hopeful call. In that time, much happened.

Amelia and Michael put in a request for a release of the case files concerning Wendell Acton's missing persons case.

Kate had commissioned and hammered in an adorable wooden sign and established herself with a boutique online reservations coordinator. The Heirloom Inn was mostly functional and even accepting reservations, much to Kate's glee. Matt helped her a little each day, and Clara—who'd grown bored with summer already—even began pitching in with planting a small garden and repainting the guest bath. She seemed comfortable enough to be around Matt, and Amelia started to witness a budding relationship of some kind. She kept her envy at bay and focused instead on Michael and her work on the Liesel Hart inquiry, composing a thoughtful letter to Liesel and sending it through certified mail.

Megan and Brian had spent several days together in Birch Harbor before he left to return home for the work week. Things between them were awkward, and there had been several small fights. Sarah sometimes got caught in the middle, but by the time they left, there was hope.

There always was.

For her part, Amelia contacted the Birch Harbor Players. For the time being, she had no need for a significant income. She agreed with her sisters to take on the role of property manager at The Bungalows, which would net her a fraction of the income. When Clara moved out of her unit, it was open for Amelia's use, should she need it.

She might, since she'd officially decided to give it a year. In a year, Amelia would know if there was a life for her in Birch Harbor, but as she always liked to do, she gave it up to God. He'd opened a window for her, now it was time to see if she could crawl inside and make a home.

All that, of course, would depend on her ability to settle into a meaningful job at minimum. Beyond the housing and a satisfying gig, all Amelia needed was a loving relationship.

Out of all three of her basic needs, the relationship was her hottest lead. In fact, that very evening, Michael was due to pick her up from the Heirloom Inn and take her out to an early dinner and then the Birch Harbor Players' first show of the season, set in a grassy park just outside of town. It was a new production based on the founding of Birch Harbor. Amelia was interested to see what events the director chose to highlight and how the company would pull off what very well could be a tiresome story. Mostly, though, Amelia was anxious to be with Michael and *not*, for once, discuss her family. It would be her first *real* date in a *long* time. And the best part? It wasn't with a twenty-something out-of-work actor. It was with a lawyer. A *man*. A friend.

At just before four, she perched at the parlor window in the Inn. Kate was upstairs, turning a bed for a couple who'd made reservations for the evening and were expected any time now. Downstairs, it was just Dobi and Amelia. They were playing a little game. Who would show up first? Michael? Or Kate's guests?

Amelia predicted it would be the guests, which left Dobi with Michael for a bet, but they were both wrong.

Outside, just beyond the white picket fence, the mail truck pulled up, popped open the mailbox and hastily slid a packet of envelopes inside. As the carrier drove off, the mailbox door fell open.

Amelia sighed and pushed up from the window seat before heading to the door. Dobi picked up her energy and darted out through the door before she could stop him and nearly ran right into the street and in front of a slowly oncoming truck.

"*Dobi!*" she screamed. The Weiner dog put on the brakes and veered left, cut off by the closed gate, anyway. Amelia laughed and shook her head then looked up to the truck. It was Michael. He stopped and popped out, closing the door behind him and pointing to the mailbox.

"Can I grab that for you?"

She smiled and nodded, disappointed that she didn't have a chance to open the door and impress him with her cobalt blue sundress.

But he was impressed even without the dramatic effect. "You look amazing."

She opened the white gate and let him in as Dobi darted around like a maniac. Michael wore khaki shorts and an easy white polo, which cut across his fit shape so beautifully she wanted to press her hands to his torso. She refrained, of course, thanked him for the compliment and returned it in kind, accepting a light peck on the cheek.

Something in her stomach stirred, but she pushed it down as deep as it would go. Tonight was not about Amelia reclaiming her youth or vying for the role of ingenue in the latest promising off-Broadway production of a Shakespearean comedy. It was about good choices. Great ones, even.

"Here you go." He passed her the mail, and she fumbled it for a moment then dropped her hand and called Dobi over. After tossing the mail on the reception desk and calling out to Kate that she was leaving, Amelia stepped back outside and caught Michael studying the marina.

"Beautiful, right?"

"Yes," he agreed, smiling.

He held out his hand, and she took it. Together they walked down the round cobblestone pavers, but Michael stopped suddenly, just before the gate. "Oops," he said, bending to collect a letter that must have slipped from his grip. "Sorry about that. Want me to run it inside?"

She plucked it from his hand and shook her head. Nothing was going to delay this moment any longer. "No, it's fine," she replied, slipping the stark white envelope into her purse with little more than a peek. It was addressed to The Hannigan Family in a lilting, sad sort of script. Likely a belated condolence card. Amelia pushed it out of her head and accepted Michael's gentlemanly help with hoisting herself into the passenger seat.

The show was odd, as many low-budget productions often were, particularly ones written and produced by the very small-town people who put them on stage. Amelia pointed out various errors in the history of the town in brief whispers with Michael who acted decidedly more respectful, keeping utterly silent through the show and joining the standing ovation after.

They walked back to his truck, hand in hand. He complimented the courage of the actors, the gorgeous green setting, and wondered what else was in store from the Birch Harbor summer stock.

Amelia liked that about him, his positivity and kindness toward the artists. She might do well to have followed suit and, indeed, once they were driving away from the park, mused that she had reached out to their director in search of a role within the company. Her experience would be a benefit to the troop and their humbleness would be a benefit to her. Michael encouraged her warmly, offering to help connect her however he could. She thanked him and wondered if he, too, might want to involve himself more. He'd make a fabulous dramaturg, she argued. He didn't know what that was, and when they laughed together it was decided they shared that in common, an eye for history.

"It's a little early still," he said after they agreed it was the next logical step that both Michael and Amelia committed to work with the Birch Harbor Players.

Amelia glanced at the clock. "You're right. Maybe we could take a little detour?"

He looked over at her and smirked.

"Hey, now," she admonished in a semi-serious tone. "I just meant a little drive."

"Ah," he replied, mock disappointment filling his voice. "That sounds nice."

In silence, they drove north for a few miles, passing by farmland intermixed with forest. "You know," Amelia said, narrowing her eyes on the mile markers and county signage. "I think our property is out here somewhere."

"What property is that?" he asked, frowning, but then answered his own question. "Oh, right. The land. From Nora's will. Do you know exactly where?"

She shook her head. "I didn't come with Megan and Kate when they made the drive to walk it. Wait!" She sliced a finger through the air at a green clearing. "There it is!"

A small wooden sign hid among a grove of white birches. He slowed down in time for Amelia to make out the words. "*Hannigan Field.*"

"Want me to turn in?"

"Sure," she replied. They drove up a gravelly, weedy lane and took in the expanse of land. It would make a perfect little event venue or perhaps dairy farm. Lots of garden space and privacy. Perfect for parties or weddings.

"It's gorgeous," Amelia said, rolling down her window and breathing in the fresh Michigan night air. "I bet the fireflies here are *amazing*," she gushed.

He laughed. "That's true. We'd have to wait until dark though, and our dinner reservation is for six-thirty."

"I can think of another place we could visit," she offered, smiling coyly.

"Let me see if I can guess," Michael said, making a smooth U-turn and pulling out of the secluded side street and back onto the thoroughfare.

Amelia smiled the whole ride, safe in the knowledge that she was with someone who, despite the short time they'd spent together, *knew* her. Truly knew her.

"Tell me about yourself, Michael," she murmured, her hand hitting air pockets out the open window.

He didn't put up a wall. He didn't change the conversation or go on about exes he hated or jobs he couldn't keep. Instead, he told her the sweet story of a city boy who longed for the country life. A quiet, country life filled with books and good meals. He confessed that despite his age, he hoped to one day marry. Maybe have a child, maybe not. He enjoyed mass on Sundays and helping people on weekdays. Saturdays were for culture, he told her. Amelia liked everything he had to say, even if it stood in stark contrast to every way she had lived her life.

By the time he finished, they'd pulled off the road and driven a mile toward the shore, parking finally just outside of the lighthouse. "Did I bore you?" he asked, glancing over at her assuredly.

"Quite the opposite," she answered. "You enchanted me." They sat in silence, staring at the narrow tower that descended high above the water like it was reaching for Heaven. But when she looked over at him, he grinned back at her.

"No one has ever called me enchanting before," he remarked, chuckling.

She laughed, too. "No one has ever enchanted me before."

Michael licked his lips, his smile falling from his mouth as he leaned over towards her. Amelia swallowed and leaned into him, pressing her hand down onto her handbag, accidentally knocking it to the floor of the truck.

The moment caught in the air, and she stared at the bag. Unreasonably bothered. "I'm sorry," she whispered, bending to collect it.

He reached for her hand and pulled her back up to him, wrapping his other hand around the back of her head and gently, slowly pulling her in for a chaste, tender kiss.

It was the most passionate moment of Amelia's life.

Just a moment later, when he took her hand in his and remained sitting, staring across to the house and lake beyond, she let out a long sigh. "I'll miss this place."

"You can come here anytime, though. Right?" He looked at her and squeezed her hand.

"I sort of... I sort of thought I'd *get* it, you know? That it could be *my* little project."

"Maybe it still can. Maybe Liesel will sell it to you."

Amelia did not want to talk about Liesel. She'd spent the past fourteen days obsessing over why she hadn't gotten a call or a text. There must have been a mistake. That's what she finally settled on. Maybe Gene was even wrong. Or maybe the so-called baby had passed away in some tragic accident. Amelia couldn't cling to the past any more than she could plan for the future. It was just her cross to bear. To roll with the punches.

"I haven't even heard from her, though," she answered, rolling her shoulders back and down. But the idea reminded her. "Wait a second," she said, releasing Michael's hand and reaching for the contents that spilled out of her bag.

His eyes lit up in the orange light of evening. "Is that what I—"

She tucked her hair behind her ears and pulled the white envelope onto her lap. "It couldn't be," she reasoned. "There's no way."

But she pinched the corner and tore it off, then pushed the side of her finger along the short end, at last pulling out a two-page handwritten letter.

Amelia's eyes flashed over the words, reality coalescing around her. "Oh my goodness," she whispered. "We were *right*." Her voice rose. "It's *her!*"

Michael leaned over and read at her side.

Amelia stuck her hand into her handbag and called Kate, adding in Clara and Megan to the line in one big group phone call. Once her sisters were all listening in, Amelia began. "You're not going to believe this."

***

After she finished relaying the new information, she looked over at Michael, who'd picked up the envelope she let drop to the console. It was an oversized white mailer, its paper thick and lined like specialty stationary.

"Look," he said, opening his hand. In it, lay a small, silver key.

"Cancel dinner," Amelia answered, plucking it from his palm. "Our plans have changed."

Chapter 40—Amelia

"Wait a minute," Amelia whispered as they neared the little home that stretched into the lighthouse building.

Michael stopped. They stood on the sand, her left hand in his right, the sun dipping lower and lower. Time felt irrelevant and relevant all at once. She could camp there that night. She could slip inside to the home of her grandparents and fall asleep to the rhythm of the lake. She could take a midnight stroll up into the tower and look out across the water and down the shore toward the Village and Heirloom Island. And she could do it all with a handsome, smart, able-bodied lawyer right there by her side.

But of course, they were losing light.

"Should we start here or there?" she waved a hand from the house to the tower.

Michael looked down at her, his eyes shimmering against the setting sun, his skin warm in the red glow. "It's your choice. I'm just here for you."

She smiled and nodded, then led him to the house where she slid the key into the lock. It fit and a gentle turn offered smooth egress. No need to break in. The house, according to Liesel, was hers to explore. And her sisters, but on the phone, they gave Amelia full permission to look around without them. After all, it would seem that they wouldn't need permission, soon enough. Soon enough, all the Hannigans could converge on the property, adding it to their growing list of projects.

The space was nearly barren. A potbellied stove squatted in the easement between a front room, perhaps a sitting room, and the kitchen where there sat an antique refrigerator and a block of wood atop iron bars—an island. It looked much different than Amelia recalled from her childhood. Smaller, sure, but also *older*. More bizarre. It reminded her of Edgar Allan Poe's birth home, which she'd visited in Philadelphia some years earlier, during a brief stint with the City Theatre as a spotlight tech. She realized now just how much Grandma Acton had done with the place.

There were just two bedrooms, which sat on either side of the small bathroom where Amelia once took a bubble bath. The same clawfoot tub from her youth still sat there. However, it had seen better days. Orange rust stains coagulated in the drain and around the hardware. A crack rang along the far lip. The pedestal sink was in similar condition. An oval mirror—no medicine cabinet—hung above, revealing a fresh-faced, awestruck woman. Amelia, of course. The mirror was cloudy with grime and age, but she liked the way she looked in it. She saw herself differently there. Happy, perhaps. Interested. Entirely consumed by where life had taken her.

"It looks like they had it cleared out," Michael commented, poking his head into a narrow linen closet. The white interior paint cracked where the hinges creaked.

Though there wasn't much to see, they spent a while examining everything from the worn shag carpet in the bedrooms to the jammed casement windows.

"It's probably just paint," Michael offered, studying the edges. "I don't see any locks."

Amelia nodded then strode back toward the front door. "Come on," she urged. "I want to go up before the sun sets."

They had time. Lord knows they had time. Summer in the northern states saw long days. Its sun sank slowly, taunting children long after their bedtime. And Amelia wanted every minute with that lazy sun. She wanted to see what was *in* there. She wanted all of it. The sun through the lighthouse windows on her skin. A chance to see Michael in that light, way high above the reflections of the lake.

He followed her from the house down the winding path of crumbling steppingstones. Though the Actons had died only relatively recently, it was now clear to Amelia that neither they nor Liesel had ever completed any renovation projects. But Amelia liked that. She wasn't too interested in turning the place into something flashy. Preservation felt more appropriate there. Some special touches, perhaps. New paint. Scrubbed porcelain. What would bring that property back to life had nothing to do with shabby chic window treatments or stainless-steel appliances. *People. People* would bring it back to life.

Amelia opened her hand to Michael, who dug the key from his pocket and passed it to her in one fluid motion. Again, she slid it into the brass lock and turned it until a satisfying click drowned out the sound of blood rushing to her head. The moment belonged to Amelia. As much as the house on the harbor belonged to Kate. As much as the cottage belonged to Clara.

She turned and glanced up at Michael, who nodded her in. The space was sparser than the house, with aged wood boards nailed in dizzying rows around the circular walls inside the ground floor. Metal ladders zigzagged up and up, narrowing away from Amelia and Michael's place on the cobblestone floor.

Amelia frowned. "I'm not sure what I was expecting." She stepped up to the windowless wall, pressing a hand to the boards as if to take the pulse of her grandfather's place. It occurred to her that she and her sisters had little stake in the property. They hardly knew their grandparents, and their father—though he did work in the lighthouse as a young man—had left it behind once he met Nora.

That didn't mean Amelia and her sisters couldn't reconnect in some way. Now more than ever she felt in her heart that there was something there, on that abandoned property. A life force of some kind.

"Take your time," Michael cautioned as Amelia mounted the first ladder.

She paused, realizing she wore a dress. "Maybe you should go first?"

He cleared his throat. "It's safer if I'm beneath you. So that I can catch you if you fall."

Amelia's cheeks glowed. Michael was a true gentleman. She could trust him. With her decency, for one, and her life, for another. She smiled down at him and began her climb. Moving like a cat from the first ladder to the second without a hitch. Michael stayed half a ladder's length below.

When she reached the top, through a hole that opened onto a sturdy platform, her breath caught in her throat.

Standing there, by the defunct red light, a view to the world awaited them. Michael's head appeared in the opening, and she reached down, taking his hand once he was in a position to push up.

"Wow." He patted his hands off on his pants and studied the light. "I've never been in a lighthouse."

"I was here a couple of times," Amelia replied. "As a girl." But it was different. "I was always distracted, though."

"What do you mean?"

"Well, you know. If we were here, we were playing around and getting into trouble. Grandpa Acton never let us come up here. I'd snuck up here." She smiled behind a faint blush.

Michael smiled at her. "You're rebellious?"

"Used to be. Megan and I were both the black sheep of the family. Until Kate surprised everyone."

"How can there be three black sheep in one family?"

Amelia frowned and strode past each window, her hand pressing along the cloudy glass as though she was testing it out for fortitude. "Good question. I guess none of us were *truly* rebels or black sheep or whatever. But when we came back here and Dad was gone... things *changed*. Our mother changed. Her temper was short. We were always grounded. Clara was her priority, which I understand now, but if Dad—"

She broke off and tears welled along her lower lash lines.

Michael walked to her, gently slipping her hand into his. He didn't finish her sentence for her. He didn't shush her or tell her not to cry. He just waited. He gave her time. He let her be.

Finally, she emerged from the darkness of her grief. "If our dad were around, maybe everything would have been normal again."

"I'm sure he wanted to be," Michael offered, his voice low.

Amelia blinked and looked up at him. "If I knew that, I think I'd be able to get over it."

"You can know that," Michael answered.

She frowned at him, confused.

He explained. "I'm not a father, but I'm a man. And I have a family. And what family man doesn't want to be with his family?"

She shrugged and stared out the window across the water. The image of her father's wristwatch flashed in her mind, and her gaze danced down below, to the dock where they'd found it. In a way, she believed Michael. "We will never have the answer, I guess," she murmured, her eyes fixed on the narrow wooden platform where her dad used to tie off.

"Amelia," Michael said, turning to face her. He let go of her hand and gripped her shoulders softly but with a purpose. He had her full attention. "You will have the answer one day. We'll find out exactly what happened to your dad. But even when we do, it won't change what you know in your heart."

The point radiated through her body, from her fingertips into her heart like a shock wave. Michael was right. No matter what became of Wendell Acton—if he got scared off by Kate's pregnancy (which she knew wasn't true), if he and their mother had a blowout fight, or if he learned about Gene—it would never strip her of the memories she did have.

The ballet classes he'd driven Amelia to when no one else in the family took her seriously about honing her dance technique. The Tragedy and Comedy faces he found at the swap meet and brought home for her. Then, of course, the week they drove to Detroit together. A father-daughter duo on the run from nothing and everything.

Just months before Kate's news, Amelia had begged their mother to take her to an oddball city tour her middle school drama teacher had raved about. The drive was long, and the whole thing sounded weird to Nora. But Wendell had interrupted their conversation about it. Amelia could just picture him, strolling into the kitchen, jangling the change in his pocket before pulling a gallon of milk from the fridge and taking an inconspicuous sip.

"You want to see a show in Detroit?" He hadn't heard her question, but his guess warmed her heart.

Nora had been working on bills, her glance toward him was both hopeful and skeptical. Amelia's gaze flew to her father, and she nodded urgently. "But it's not really a show, it's a walking tour of downtown Detroit. But Mr. Adamski said that if you grow up in Michigan, it's just one of those things you have to do."

"It sounds dangerous," Nora had inserted, finally pausing and giving the request its due attention. "Downtown Detroit? And, come on. That would be true of, oh, I don't know. Frankenmuth, that adorable little German town. Or Mackinac Island. Or the Tulip festival, for Heaven's sake. But a walking tour of downtown? This isn't New York." She laughed and returned to her noisy adding machine, the white paper curling down the side of the table.

Amelia remembered feeling a deep disappointment. As a child, before that summer trip to the wild west, Amelia's idea of her future felt fuzzy but optimistic. She could be anything. She always thought that. She could be a veterinarian or a teacher or a doctor, if she wanted.

"I can handle a little danger," Wendell answered, winking at Amelia. Her love for her father had swelled like a balloon. "And anyway," he'd added, "I love local history."

Now Michael's words swirled in her head like a tornado. He was right. It didn't matter where he went. Amelia knew that Wendell Acton was a good dad. A great one. He loved her sisters and her mother. And he loved Amelia. More than any man ever would, probably.

She glanced up to Michael, swallowing past the lump in her throat. "Thank you," she whispered and pushed up on the balls of her feet, closing her eyes and trusting that he felt the same.

Michael kissed her softly, with patience. He kissed her slowly, so that she could shake her worries about the past and fears about the future. He transported her into a fairytale but kept her grounded there, on the observation deck, surrounded by the slow sunset and glistening water. Surrounded, too, by the promise of a fresh start.

In the lighthouse on the lake, Amelia was everything she ever wanted to be. She was her father's daughter. She was a princess in a tower with her unwitting knight in shining armor. She wasn't *in* the spotlight, of course. Instead, she *was* the spotlight.

But, mostly, Amelia was *home*.

Epilogue

Megan Stevenson clicked off the call and turned to Brian. They were eating dinner together, as had become a new, odd tradition, especially with Sarah spending her summer in Birch Harbor with Clara. It was late June, and though the divorce paperwork still existed, it was firmly on hold.

They were trying to make things work. In the weeks since their initial reunion, as Kate's first official guests at the Heirloom Inn, Hannigan history had finally settled into place.

The letter from Liesel confirmed Amelia's suspicions to the T. In the summer of 1992—the summer they'd spent in Arizona—Liesel had turned twenty-seven. She was on the brink of a personal crisis, coming to terms with learning that she was adopted through her loudmouth younger brother. In an effort to know everything she could, she tracked down contact information for her birth mother. The only trouble was that a firm no-contact order still stood in place, despite Liesel's age. Her mother, a woman named Nora Hannigan, had signed paperwork preventing Liesel from ever reaching out. Still determined, Liesel went against her nature and the order and called Nora's home phone number. It had gone to voicemail. Afraid to leave a message regarding such a big thing, Liesel instead wrote down the name from the machine's greeting. *Hi! You've reached Nora and Wendell. We're out right now. Leave a message, and we'll call you back!*

Wendell Hannigan. On a whim, Liesel had called for information about a Wendell Hannigan who lived in the area code of the phone number. Luck struck, and she spoke with someone, a local fisherman who knew a Wendell, but his name was Wendell Acton. This, somehow, made even more sense to Liesel. Surely if she was given up by these people, they might have a rocky history. Or perhaps she wasn't even his child, but he could at least point her to Nora.

By the time she had tracked down Wendell Acton's parents—who could have been *her* grandparents, he was gone. Off the map.

But by then, Liesel learned that Wendell Acton's parents worked the lighthouse north of Birch Harbor, Michigan. All it took was a phone call, one rainy Saturday. They answered and when Liesel so much as suggested that she may have been Wendell Acton's long-lost daughter, they believed her without question. It confirmed for Liesel all she had hoped for. However, the Actons warned Liesel away from Nora, claiming she had moved on and wasn't worth the emotional energy.

Still, Liesel and her paternal grandparents stayed in close touch. And when they passed, they requested the deed to the lighthouse be transferred to one Liesel Hart of Hickory Grove, Indiana.

She had no idea that she had younger sisters. She had no idea that Nora's heart was shattered at losing her.

And she had no idea what she was going to do with the lighthouse on the lake because she had just recently inherited her own piece of family history, two properties in her *hometown*.

When Liesel, on the phone with Amelia and Megan and Kate and Clara, had used that phrase, they knew that things would fall into place. That they could accept that Liesel, though their sister in blood, had her own life. That she was doing as well as they were. And, in fact, Liesel offered to transfer the deed to the Hannigans. But that wasn't all. Included in her envelope was the key to the lighthouse. It was a gesture of sisterhood and of family and one of a promise that one day, they would have a great big Hannigan reunion in the lighthouse on the lake.

Now, as Megan scraped the last of the ice cream from her bowl, her phone flashed alive. A text from Sarah with an image.

Megan flipped it over and studied it. There her sister stood, in the doorway of the attached home on the lighthouse, a broad paint brush in one hand and a sloppy paint bucket dangling from the other. Michael was in the picture, too, staring down at Amelia with a look of love that Megan admired so. They were a great couple, and she would know. He wielded a hammer, and around his waist was a leather apron with other tools sticking out at odd angles.

Behind the camera was Megan and Brian's daughter, happy to be part of a great, big, messy family for a summer on the shore. Megan smiled and read Sarah's message.

Just you wait! Birch Harbor is getting a museum! Aunt Amelia said I can work here until it's time to go back to school!

Brian interrupted her with a loud gulp of water. In the past, the habit was a pet peeve of hers. Now, she tried to embrace it as one of the sounds of her life, of her marriage. "Have you heard back about that job yet?" His voice was gentle, but the words cut through her heart.

"Yes." Megan had applied for a position in Detroit at Make Me a Match, a service for senior citizens who were looking for love in their golden years. Well, technically, she emailed them and suggested they develop a new position.

"And?" he pressed, biting his lower lip.

"They aren't interested in a social media manager after all. I guess their demographic is looking for something else." She sighed and rubbed the back of her neck.

A sly smile spread across his face. "Have you ever thought of starting your own company?"

***

I hope you enjoyed Lighthouse on the Lake. *The next story in this saga is* Fireflies in the Field, *available widely.*

Other Titles by Elizabeth Bromke

Birch Harbor:
House on the Harbor
Fireflies in the Field
Hickory Grove:
The Schoolhouse
The Christmas House
The Farmhouse
The Innkeeper's House
Maplewood:
Christmas on Maplewood Mountain
Return to Maplewood
Missing in Maplewood
The Billionaire's Mountain Bride
The Ranger's Mountain Bride
The Cowboy's Mountain Bride

Acknowledgements

I started writing this book during a family trip to Disneyland. It was the best vacation I've been on. My husband planned it with enthusiasm and heart, and every moment was magical, especially the whole "seeing it through my son's eyes." It took my breath away, in fact.

As I write my thank yous, the world has morphed into something out of a post-apocalyptic science fiction. The Coronavirus has brought us to our knees. People have fallen sick and died. Half the world or more has lost employment. Businesses have shuttered and National Parks have closed in an effort to slow the spread of a new and vicious virus. Healthcare workers, scientists, and our essential workforce are standing in the way of certain doom and offering us hope. You are our heroes.

No matter whether we're braving exposure to fill prescriptions or huddling at home, afraid to tear our eyes away from the news, we're stressed. I've been stressed. And yet, I have my readers. My friends! I see you on social media and in my email. I see you in my reviews. I see what escaping in a book means for others (not just me). Thank you. Thank you for reminding me how much we need the distraction of far-away stories to cope.

A huge thanks to Wilette Cruz, who put together gorgeous design. Lisa Lee and Krissy Moran: you're also weathering the storm of COVID, but you're still there for me. Thank you. For your patience and flexibility and prowess. Thank you!

My advanced readers are invaluable to my process. Without you, I would not publish. Thank you!

Mom and Dad, thank you for always believing in me. Your support of my creative spirit has been crucial. To all my family, thank you.

Ed, thank you for encouraging and inspiring me. Little E., you too. Through it all, I love being stuck at home with my two favorite guys.